Looks Aren't Everything

"Shallow girls do. Like me. I'm shallow too. I know it. But I don't mind. To me it's a compliment. Life is short, Jeanie, and short means shallow. I don't need deep conversations. I don't need profound thoughts. I don't need meaningful meetings. I like simple things. I like handsome boys. That's what I like. That's what pleases me. That's what fills me with admiration for the world. Handsome boys. I mean, what else is there when you get right down to it? What else is there worthy of a girl's own love? The love of a handsome boy, that's what. Really."

LOOKS AREN'T EVERYTHING

J. D. Landis

BANTAM BOOKS

NEW YORK · TORONTO · LONDON · SYDNEY · AUCKLAND

RL 6, age 12 and up

LOOKS AREN'T EVERYTHING

A BANTAM BOOK

Bantam hardcover edition / March 1990
Bantam paperback edition / March 1991

*The Starfire logo is a registered trademark of Bantam Books, a division
of Bantam Doubleday Dell Publishing Group, Inc. Registered in U.S. Patent
and Trademark Office and elsewhere.*

ISBN 0-553-28860-1

Published simultaneously in the United States and Canada

---

*Bantam Books are published by Bantam Books, a division of Bantam Doubleday
Dell Publishing Group, Inc. Its trademark, consisting of the words "Bantam
Books" and the portrayal of a rooster, is Registered in U.S. Patent and
Trademark Office and in other countries. Marca Registrada. Bantam Books,
666 Fifth Avenue, New York, New York 10103.*

PRINTED IN THE UNITED STATES OF AMERICA

OPM   0 9 8 7 6 5 4 3 2

For my mother,
Eve S. Landis

LOOKS AREN'T

EVERYTHING

1

Whenever I had a problem with boys, I talked to my best friend, Jeanie.

It's not that Jeanie had so many boyfriends. She didn't have *any*. But she did have a brother, which was more than I could say. A very beautiful brother.

"I don't know a thing about boys," she'd tell me.

"But you must. You have a brother." Needless to say, I didn't add anything about his beauty. In my life, boys came after *me*.

But Jeanie was right. She didn't know a thing about boys. Which still didn't stop me from going to her with my problems. I didn't need her answers. I just needed to talk to her in order to be able to hear myself. That's what friends are for.

Jeanie worked after school and on weekends at the Plainview Mall. Her parents leased one of those many-sided stands right in the middle of a huge corridor, with The Dog Pound on one side of them and Nuts From All Nations on the other. Jeanie's family sold all sorts of strange things that I always thought nobody would ever buy.

Belt buckles that said, *Plainview. Home of the Hogs.*

Earrings that spelled *Left* and *Right*.

Pins with pictures of James Dean, and Elvis, and Dolly Parton, and one of Michael Jackson and Elizabeth Taylor out on a date.

Tie clasps that were tiny sculptures of women in bikinis—I mean, who would buy such things!

Leather moccasins that had one tag that said, *Made by Genuine Indians* and another, tinier tag that said, *Hecho in Taiwan.*

Mr. and Mrs. Higgins, Jeanie Higgins, and Handsome Harry Higgins, as her brother was known, were all locked in the middle of the huge Plainview Mall in their tiny shop called La Maison de Trash. For me it was just like the world itself—la maison de trash. They were always bumping into one another. There were always customers looking for strange things. It was very hectic.

"All I want is to be alone," Jeanie would say. "I've had enough people to last me a lifetime."

My own problem was just the opposite. I didn't have much of a family left. Not only was I an only child, but my parents had divorced four years ago when I was twelve. When I was home there was only me and my mom. It was quiet. It was intimate. It was really dull.

Maybe that's why I had always had a date with one boy or another. One after the other. And Jeanie had never had one. She said that growing up with a brother was enough to cure any girl of boys forever. She couldn't wait until Harry graduated. She hoped he would ship out in the Navy or get a job modeling in New York or decide to go to college at the University of Northern Alaska, if there were such a place.

She said she didn't understand a thing about boys and didn't want to.

My problem was the same and the opposite. I didn't understand a thing about boys . . . and there was nothing else in the world I wanted to know.

2

Jeanie was selling a short man a ceramic statue of an Indian smoking a peace pipe when I burst into La Maison de Trash and breathlessly said, "I can't believe this is happening to me!"

"Hello, Rosie," said Mr. Higgins calmly. He was doing inventory or something. But then he always seemed to be doing inventory. I think he just loved to handle that stuff.

"Hi, Mr. Higgins."

"Jeanie's busy right now. She's selling a *Chief Talking Bull.*"

Jeanie looked over at me and winked. Her customer was handling the statue of the Indian as if it were *The Thinker.*

"Did I hear you say you can't believe what is happening to you?" asked Mrs. Higgins. "Boy trouble again?"

"Am I that predictable?"

She laughed. She was heavyset with an enormous chest.

Sometimes I wished she were my own mother and I could just put my head down on her and she would put her hand in my golden hair over my ear and the only thing I'd be able to hear would be her soothing wisdom. This woman had a daughter *and* a son. There wasn't anything she didn't seem to know.

"Of course you are," she answered. "I just wish Jeanie were, too."

"Were what?" asked Harry, who didn't look at us because he was keeping his eyes peeled for customers. It was just as well. I didn't like Harry to look at me, even though I wanted him to. He was too good-looking for his own good. And certainly for mine. I'd known Harry since I was four and he was six. For all those twelve years, I'd never been able to figure him out. And I'd never been able to stop wanting to figure him out. He was the boy I'd known the longest and the boy I knew the least. He was the biggest mystery of them all.

"I was just saying that I wish Jeanie were predictable enough to have boy troubles," said Mrs. Higgins. "Like Rosie here."

Now Harry turned and looked at me. There was a strange expression in his eyes. He didn't seem to know me. I wondered if he were seeing me for the first time and wishing it were the last.

"*You* have boy troubles?" he asked.

His sarcasm thrilled me. He'd never spoken to me like that before. We'd never really had much of a relationship. He kept away from "the girls" when we were together. I'd only been Jeanie's best friend. I'd always figured he'd seen me as a kind of sister, once removed. But now he didn't seem to like me at all. The odd thing was that suddenly I wanted Harry to like me. The thought startled me. Did I really want to be wanted by Handsome Harry Higgins, my best friend's brother? How trite!

But did he want me now that he seemed to notice me?

Or did he genuinely find me a nuisance? I didn't care about what he wanted really. I decided Harry had better want me. Who wouldn't?

I was desperate to find out.

"Believe it or not I have capital B-O-Y trouble." I gave him sarcasm for sarcasm.

"You look like *girl* trouble."

"I am," I snapped back. I didn't even know what I was saying. Was I trouble to boys? Or was I just trouble for myself? What was Harry really thinking?

"I pity your boyfriend," Harry said.

That did it. He obviously was a snide wise guy without taste. "Which one?" I asked sweetly.

"Which *one?*"

That's when I saw his face change. Did he seem jealous? Was I imagining things?

"How many do you *have?*" he asked.

"That depends on whether you count Ron Falsey."

"Ron Falsey!"

"Or Gene Stemkowski."

"Gene Stemkowski!"

"Or Bull Francis."

"Bull Francis!"

"Or Lester Cousins."

"Lester Cousins! He's—"

"Or—"

"What is this, the whole Plainview High football team? You *do* have a problem if you're dating the whole—"

"Just kidding," I said. "The truth is . . ."

"Just what *is* the truth?" Harry asked.

The truth was, he had me totally confused. Every once in a while it occurred to me that I was in love with Harry. But that's what's supposed to happen with your best friend's older brother. You're in love with him because he's cute and he never pays the least attention to you. Nothing happens.

Your friendship isn't ruined. But what happens when he gets sarcastic and starts to make fun of you?

Why, your heart takes a leap and your brain does a cartwheel.

You realize that just maybe this guy, who you've known for practically your whole life, might care about you enough to think you're ridiculous.

I didn't know what to do now. Fortunately, I was rescued when a customer appeared and Harry turned away.

"Can I help you?" he asked.

"Do you have a childproof bottle opener?" asked the man. "My kids keep opening my beers."

"Of course we do," said Harry, and he showed the man a bottle opener in the shape of a woman.

"Rescue me," I whispered toward Jeanie.

As if she could read my mind, she handed her customer his *Chief Talking Bull* statue and his change and hurried toward me saying, "You can't believe *what* is happening to you?"

3

"I'll be back soon," Jeanie called as we left the rest of the Higginses in La Maison de Trash and started to stroll through the mall. We held arms, like women in foreign movies. It made our revelations all the more intimate.

The strangest thing of all about the mall was how it made me feel I wasn't even part of my world. I felt so free when I was there. I could say anything. And I usually did.

I didn't want to go shopping. I just wanted to talk. So I pulled Jeanie along with me and headed for the far end of the mall, miles away.

"The thing I can't believe is happening to me is how the wrong guys keep asking me for dates."

"Like who?" asked Jeanie as we both let our eyes scan the carousels of sale shoes sitting outside Heel 'n' Toe.

"Well, Jack Trumbull asked me to go to the movies on Saturday."

"Ugh, Jack Trumbull." Jeanie wrinkled her nose. "What movie?"

"Get this. He wants to see *Top Gun* for the seventy-third time."

"Typical." Jeanie waved her hand in the air as if Jack Trumbull were a gnat flying between our heads. "Who else?"

"Bruce Ashworth told me he wants to play his guitar for me. At his house. In the basement."

"Bruce Ashworth. I remember when his name was Paul. Does he still call himself 'The Boss'?"

"Don't you know it!"

Together, we laughed at Bruce. He'd changed his name from Paul to Bruce, taken up the guitar, and went around singing songs he'd written about the bowling alleys and pizza shops of Plainview.

"Who else?"

"Well," I said, steering us toward the Potato Man stand, "Steve Pease absolutely begged me to go with him to see an exhibition of his mother's paintings."

"Mrs. Pease! I know her paintings. She tried to get us to sell them at La Maison. My father said no way, José."

"Why not?"

"They were junk. Absolute junk."

"No *way* they belonged at La Maison de Trash then."

"No *way*." Jeanie raised her hands for me to slap them. "But I can't believe she got a gallery to handle them," she went on.

"It's not a gallery. The exhibition is in the Pease living room."

"La Maison de Travesty."

I pulled her with me. "That deserves a stuffed potato skin. What'll it be?"

We didn't even have to look at the illuminated Potato Man menu.

"Sour cream and applesauce," she said to the guy behind the counter, who was dressed up as a potato, right down to the wiry root-hairs sprouting from his forehead and the warts on his nose.

"Wheat germ and apple pectin for me," I said.

"Anything to drink?" asked the potato.

"Two potato juices," I said.

"Carbonated or flat?"

"Need you ask? Don't we eat here often enough? Flat, my man. Flat." I gave him my stuffiest tone of voice.

"Well, excuuuuuuuse me," he said. "I'm new here."

"Well, how were we supposed to know that?" Jeanie asked. "You look just like the other potatoes."

"Of course I look just like the other potatoes. I'm wearing the same uniform."

"You mean that's not how you look naturally?" I teased him. "I thought that's how you got a job at this place. I thought it was a requirement that you look like a potato. I mean, I had no idea those were *uniforms.*"

"What's the matter, you don't like the way I look?" he asked.

"You're ugly," I said. Then I realized that wasn't really fair. So I added, "I don't mean *you're* ugly. I mean, maybe you *are* ugly. But I don't know. What I do know is that you're *dressed* ugly. That uniform is—"

"Maybe I'm just not your type," said the potato. "What about you?" he asked Jeanie.

"Me? Gee, I don't know. You certainly look different. Maybe even cute."

"Cute?" I couldn't believe it. No wonder Jeanie never went out. She had the taste of a fruit fly. How could the guy beneath all that ugliness respect her judgment if she tried to flatter him by calling him cute in his potato incarnation? Unless, of course, he was even uglier for real than he was as a potato.

"Thanks," he said to her. "I appreciate it. Now that'll be five sixty-seven for the potato skins." He held out his gargantuan potato mitten.

"My treat." I gave him six dollars. "Keep the change."

He shook his potato head. "No tipping. See the sign? No tipping. But I'll tell you what—how about going out with me?"

"What?" I said.

"Not another one," said Jeanie.

"See what I mean," I said to her. "I walk around the mall, and a potato asks me out on a date."

We had a good shriek over that. And when we were finished, the potato said, "Not you. *Her*."

Jeanie looked around. "Who?"

"You," he said.

"Me? I don't date. Not even boys. Human beings."

"All the more reason," he said. "Date a potato. It's Date-a-Potato Month."

"You've got to be kidding," she said. "Who are you, anyway? Take that thing off for a minute."

"What you see is what you get." He bobbed his potato head around as if he were Clark Gable. "So what do you say?"

"Where's our food?" she artfully changed the subject.

"Is that to go or to stay?" asked the potato.

"To go," said Jeanie. "Definitely to go."

"Is it my warts?" he asked as he walked away to get our order.

Jeanie watched him waddle away. "It's your huge behind," she called after him.

That made him turn right around. His outfit was so big and padded that he nearly hit another potato who was carrying a load of potato skin chips. "That's because I'm a potato," he cried mournfully at Jeanie. "That's because I'm a potato."

"What do you think?" she whispered to me while he was gone.

"About what?"

"Him."

"The potato?"

"Yeah. Should I go out with him?"

I couldn't believe my ears. "Why would you go out with *him?*"

"Because he asked me. Because he *is* different."

"Oh, God, Jeanie! And I thought *I* had problems."

"You do," she said. "You do. Tell me more."

So I did, as we wandered the mall, eating our stuffed potato skins, drinking our potato juice and talking about boys and the terrible problems involved in finding the right ones to love and to get them to love us. Or me, anyway. Jeanie still didn't care for males of the human variety. Or maybe she just hadn't met the right one yet.

4

When I was done telling her about all the wrong guys who had asked me out, she said, "So it looks like you won't be dating for a while."

"Whoa." I put my hand on her arm. "Who said I wasn't dating?"

"But all those horrible guys. Jack Trumbull, Bruce Ashworth, Steve Pease, Allan Filbert, Arnie Bullock, Jeff—"

"Who said I wasn't going out with them?"

"You mean you *accepted* all those dates? You said yes to all those creeps?"

"Of course I said yes. Why else would I rush into your store screaming, 'I can't believe this is happening to me!'? Don't you see, Jeanie? Don't you understand? I'm date crazy. I'm needy. A guy asks me out and I accept. I don't care who he is. What he is. Where he wants to take me. I just don't want to be alone. I mean, I was ready to say yes to that potato back there. And I was disappointed when he said it was *you* he was asking out. Disappointed. That a potato should be asking out my best friend and not me. Date crazy! That's what I am. And I don't know what to do about it."

Jeanie looked at me as if I were some kind of nut. Then she took my head in her hands and looked me straight in the eye as if she were about to deliver the greatest piece of advice ever given by one girl to another, and she said, "That potato is *mine*."

That was all it took to clear my head. Boys! Potatoes! What was the difference? What kind of world were we living in? What was wrong with listening to Bruce (formerly Paul) Ashworth sing songs about playing Little League in Plainview, or watching Jeff Keisling pedal his ergometer until he collapsed right in front of you and that was your whole date with him?

It wasn't love. But it was life. And life went on.

"Let's shop," I said with joyful resignation. I may have screwed my life up, but I loved it just the same.

Hand in hand Jeanie and I walked into Girl Crazy.

Heads turned.

So what if they were the wrong heads?

5

So life for me went on just as it always had.

Boys kept asking me out.

But they were the wrong boys.

I kept accepting.

But I never accepted my acceptance.

Only when I got home later that afternoon did my life change. And it didn't even take a boy asking me out.

All it took was my mother coming home from work and knocking on the door of my room, where I was sitting at my desk making a list of the boys least likely to succeed at winning my heart (a list made up almost exclusively of people I'd accepted dates with).

"Come in," I said.

But she *was* in.

"Rosie," she said. "Rosie. Rosie, Rosie, Rosie."

Her cheeks were flushed. Her short, blond hair didn't

seem as perfectly in order as it usually was. And her eyes—
her calm, deep, placid, cool, faraway eyes—were burning
and intense.

She looked a little nuts.

"Hey, Mom. What's happening? You look—"

"I can't," she said and stopped either to catch her breath
or to reconsider what she had been about to say.

"You can't what?"

"I can't believe . . ."

"You can't believe what?"

"I can't believe this is happening . . ."

"What's happening?"

"I can't believe this is happening to me!"

Unbelievable. All my sympathy for my mother flew
away. "Mom, were you following me around this afternoon?"

Now she looked at me as if *I* were crazy.

"Was I what?"

"Were you listening to me, Mom? Were you bugging
my conversations?"

"Rosie, don't be absurd. I wasn't—"

"Were you by any chance dressed up like a potato and—"

"Like *what*?"

"—like a potato who asked what I thought was me but
then he said was Jeanie out on a date?"

"Yes, that's it," she said. "A date. So just who was
following whom around, young lady? Maybe *you* were following *me*."

"A potato asked you out on a date?"

My mother covered her face with her hands.

"Not a potato. Not a potato, Rosie. A man. It wasn't a
potato who asked me out on a date. And thank God is all I
can say to that. I mean, I haven't been asked out on a date
since . . . never mind when. A date. With a man. What do
you think of that? I mean, I can't believe this is happening to
me. What am I going to do, Rosie? I mean, *help*. You know
what I mean? *Help!*"

"Calm down, Mom."

She spoke from behind her hands. "Calm down. Yes. I think that's right. I think that's what I should do. Calm down." She lowered her hands. "See, I'm calmer already. I am. Look at me. I'm sitting down now. I'm sitting down and I'm composing myself." She sat down on the edge of the bed. "There. I'm composed. Almost. I'm composed except for my heart. I just can't make it stop beating."

"Thank goodness," I said.

"No, no, no. I don't mean stop beating. I mean, stop beating so *fast*. I swear, Rosie, I've been running on overdrive ever since it happened. I couldn't *wait* to get home to tell you. Feel it. Put your hand on my heart. Come over here and put your hand on my heart. You'll see what I mean. It's beating like a maniac."

"I wonder why," I said as I got up from my desk chair and went over to her.

"This whole thing is making me crazy. Here." She took my hand. "Feel."

So there we were, my mother and I, her hand over my hand, my hand over her heart.

"Feel it?"

"It's a time bomb, Mom."

"Don't joke with me, Rosie. I didn't come here for you to make fun of me. I came here to get some advice from you."

Who? Me? Some advice? My own mother coming to me for advice? About what? About *dating*? Impossible.

"Advice about what, Mom?"

"About dating, silly. What else?"

6

It was four years since my parents had gotten a divorce. My dad had moved out and then he took a job far across the country, leaving my mom and me rambling around in our big house. It was amazing how the house had never seemed all that big when my dad was living in it with us. In fact, it had always seemed somewhere between just right and too small; we were constantly running into one another wherever we went in it, and so we'd always be saying, "Hi, Mom. Hi, Rosie. Hi, Dad. Hi, Rosie." But as soon as Dad left, our house grew. It grew into a vast place full of empty, silent rooms, and the talk was cut in half. It was just, "Hi, Mom. Hi, Rosie."

It's no fun when your own home becomes a lonely place. It's enough to make you date crazy.

But I'd never figured my mother was lonely. Somehow with a parent, you figure that as long as they have *you*, why should they need anyone else? Maybe that's selfish and self-centered, but the way kids see it, why leave such behavior to adults alone?

I hated to see my mother lonely. Maybe she should never have married my father in the first place. But where would that have left me?

I wasn't one of those kids who wished she hadn't ever been born, never mind my parents' divorce or the fact that I hadn't once in my life been asked out on a date by the kind of guy I would have asked out on a date if I were the kind of girl who asked guys out on dates, if such guys could be found in Plainview or in the world in the first place, which they couldn't.

I loved life!

It was just the lonely days and lonely nights I couldn't stand.

And what was the cure for lonely days and lonely nights?

There was only one cure. It was the eternal cure.

Dating.

When I was twelve I'd realized that there was only one thing in life worth having, and that was a boyfriend who loved me and kept telling me he loved me over and over again while he got more handsome every day—and he began training the minute he became a teenager to go to business school so I wouldn't have to support him for the rest of his life, and mine.

But next to the prospect of my own Perfect Date, this was the most unusual and exciting thing I'd encountered since I turned twelve.

My mother, Ellen Dupuy, had been asked out on a date. And she'd come to me for advice.

Well, she'd come to the expert.

7

"So just what is it you want to know?" I asked as I sat down next to her on my bed. We were like two best friends, about to share the secrets of the universe. Or if not of the universe, then of the boy next door, so to speak.

"Oh, Rosie," she said, "it's not that I want to know something. Anything. Or I'm not sure what I want to know. I guess the main thing is that I just wanted to tell you. I mean, this is so *unusual*." She clapped her hands. "He asked me out on a date. Can you believe it? He asked me out on a date."

"Mom, what's so unusual about that? People get asked out on dates all the time. Take me, for instance. I—"

My mom made it instantly clear that she didn't want to talk about *my* dating. "I know about *you*, Rosie. You have more dates than a calendar. But I don't. This is new to me. I mean, it's so new, I don't even know what to do. I haven't had a date since I dated your father. And that was before you were born."

"I should hope so."

She laughed. Then her eyes kind of went back into her head. I knew she was thinking about dating my dad. Her face went limp. She was falling in love with her past.

"Snap out of it, Mom!" I gave her a shake.

She shook her head, as if to disentangle it from a spider's web. "I was just thinking about your father."

"No kidding."

"You mean you knew I was thinking about your father? Really, Rosie. Sometimes I think you can read my mind. Sometimes I think you're a genius. At least when it comes to men."

"Let's not get carried away, Mom."

She took my shoulders in both hands. And as she spoke, she shook me. "Oh, but let's, Rosie. Let's. *Let's* get carried away."

I put my hands on her hands, not just to show my support but also to make her stop shaking me. "Calm down, Mom. Take it easy. Just tell me about it. Like who is this guy?"

"Which guy?"

"The guy who asked you out, of course."

She put her hands back in her lap and lifted her head in thought. "The man who asked me out? Oh, I can't tell you that."

"Are you kidding me? What do you mean, you can't tell me that? You want my advice on dating, and you won't even tell me who it is who's asked you out on a date?"

She got her firm look on her face. She usually used it when she told me I had to be home by a certain hour or when I couldn't use her hyena placenta shampoo which was supposed to make your hair laugh according to the ads. "No, I won't tell you who asked me out."

"But why not?"

"It's private. It's between me and him. I mean, I haven't even told him whether I'll go on the date. Suppose I don't go. It would only humiliate him if people knew who he was."

"You haven't accepted yet?"

"Of course not. I—"

"Mom, take it from the expert. A guy asks you out on a date, you *always* accept."

"You do?"

"That's my philosophy."

"But I'm not sixteen, Rosie. I'm nearly . . . I'm not going to tell you."

"Mom, first you won't tell me who's the guy who asked you out. And now you're not going to tell me how old you are? Mom, I *know* how old you are."

"Nearly thirty-seven," she confessed. "Can you believe it? Me. Ellen Sanders Dupuy. Nearly thirty-seven. I'm too *old* to date. Let's face it. I'm too old to—"

"You're *not* too old. If anything, I'm too young. But we both know there's no truth to that. So if I'm not too young, then you certainly can't be too old."

My mother looked at me like my mother of old, with a smile that could almost be called wise. "I love your logic, Rosie Girl."

"Forget my logic. What about yours? What did you tell this guy when he asked you out on this date? You didn't say yes. Did you say no?"

"No, I didn't say no."

"So what *did* you tell the poor guy?"

"I told him I'd have to ask my daughter first."

8

My mother and I went out to dinner that night to discuss the situation. Actually, I took her. It wasn't something I normally did. Usually, she cooked dinner while I did my homework. Then we'd eat together, and after dinner I'd either do more homework or go out on one of my dates. My mother either watched television or did paperwork. She was a real estate agent in a large office, and there was always a lot of stuff to take care of. I didn't know how she could stand to be home all evening. Ever since my father had left, it was too quiet. It made me desperate enough to take up card games or watch TV. To my mind, the invention of television ranked right down there with food-eating contests and cheer-leading and guns as about the stupidest things ever conceived of by the human mind. I couldn't sit still long enough to watch a TV program, no matter what it was. I could hardly sit still long enough to do anything that required me to be alone and quiet. I liked to be around people. I liked people to be around me. I vowed not to sit around and vegetate like my mother.

Four whole years without a date! I couldn't say I'd ever thought about her dateless life before. But now that I had, I couldn't believe it. It was lucky she had come to me. And not a moment too soon.

We went to a place called Trattoria Freddy. It was more than I could afford but I wanted to go someplace grown-up and quiet, where we could talk and not be bothered by all the teenage screaming at the places I usually hung out.

But before we could go out, I had to break the date I had for that night.

The problem was, it was with a guy whose name I didn't know.

I'd met him for the first and only time in my life in the hallway outside English almost a week before. He came on real strong and I'd accepted for my first free night. I gave him my address and he said he'd pick me up at seven. It never even occurred to me that I didn't know his name. In my mind, all I'd thought about was my date with the guy in the pink Lacoste shirt I'd met outside English. Until I actually found out if the guy deserved to have a name—or at least a name I'd want to remember—it seemed good enough to think of him that way. But whether he'd just end up another one of those guys I went out with once and found out that he didn't have it in one of the departments that counted—looks or brains or sense of humor or courtesy or kindness or small talk or big talk or listening or no Jim McMahon imitation (not to mention no Bruce Willis imitation) or keep your hands off me or warm eyes or safe driver or no drinking or respect for his parents or no b.s. or find Rosie gorgeous— that was another question.

Not that I expected a lot from a guy. But, like all girls, I did have certain standards. So what if so far not one guy in the world had measured up to them. If somebody had, I wouldn't have had to date so many guys. And I wouldn't be in the position of not knowing the name of the guy I had to break my date with.

I called Jeanie. She was working late at the mall. "I need your help, Jeanie. I know this is a stupid question, but do you know who I'm dating tonight?"

"Do I know who you're . . . What is this, a quiz? All right. Let me see. Is it one of those guys you were telling me about this afternoon? Like Steve Pease or Jack Trumbull or—"

"No. Those are all next week. Or the week after. I forget. No, this is tonight. It's a guy I met outside English. I don't remember much about him, except he had on a pink shirt with one of those dumb alligators on it and he wouldn't take no for an answer, not that I ever offered it. I think he was new in school. Or else he's been keeping a very low profile. Of course, he was kind of cute. You know me when it comes to guys and looks. I don't know if I like dark guys or blond guys or tall guys or short guys or thin guys or muscular guys or guys with glasses or guys with ears that stick out or ears that stick in. I like *all* guys, as long as they're gorgeous. Looks are very important to me. If my heart says yes, but my eyes say no, I'll listen to my eyes."

"If you listen to your eyes, how come you can't remember who you have a date with tonight?" asked Jeanie.

"Very funny." But I wasn't hurt by her sarcasm. I always loved it when she confirmed she knew me better than I knew myself. "But do you know him?"

"I don't have the least idea who you're talking about. Is that all you know about him? He had on that pink shirt and he forced himself on you, and he's gorgeous, of course."

"Of course. And one more thing. He's a senior."

"How do you know that?"

"Because he said to me, 'I want to go out with you before it's too late.' "

"How do you know that means he's a senior?"

"Well, I don't think it meant he has a fatal disease."

Jeanie laughed. "I just don't know, Rosie. Let me ask my brother."

"Oh, no," I started to say. But it was too late. I didn't want to be embarrassed in front of Harry by not even knowing the name of the guy I had a date with. Not that I minded Harry thinking I was popular. But I wanted him to take me seriously. And even I had to admit that serious women did not have dates with people to whom they had not been properly introduced—or introduced to at all!

When Jeanie came back on the phone, she said, "His name is Barry Koontz."

"Barry Koontz. Barry Koontz." I tried to place him. I failed. "I've never heard of him. How do you *know* it's Barry Koontz?"

"Harry told me."

Harry was involved now. How appalling for my reputation. "And how does Harry know?" I asked. "Is this Barry Koontz the only guy in the school who wears a pink Lacoste?"

"Nope. Harry says he saw Barry Koontz ask you out, except he didn't know just what he was asking you, so he went up to Barry Koontz and he asked him what he was talking to you about and Barry Koontz told him that he asked you out and Harry told him he must be out of his mind."

"Oh, Jeanie, Harry said that? What a terrible thing to say. Why would Harry say a thing like that? Boys who go out with me aren't out of their minds. If anyone is out of their mind, it's me, going out with boys like Barry Koontz. I don't even know Barry Koontz. But you know what, Jeanie? Maybe I'll go out with him just to get back at Harry for saying such a terrible thing about me."

"But Rosie, I thought you *were* going out with Barry Koontz."

"No, of course not. I wouldn't need to know his name if I were going out with him. I'm *not* going out with him. And I've got to tell him I'm not going out with him, so he won't come here to pick me up and I won't be anywhere to be found. I don't stand boys *up*, you know."

"I know. But why aren't you going out with him?"

"I have another date."

"Rosie, you didn't make two dates in one night. I mean, how low can you go? But go ahead. Give me the bad news. Who is your *other* date with?"

"My mother."

"Your mother?"

"My mother."

"You're breaking a date with Barry Koontz, whoever he is, to have a date with your mother instead?"

"That's right."

"Rosie, that's the healthiest thing I've ever heard you say. I hope you have a very wonderful time."

"Thanks, Jeanie."

"Don't thank me. Thank Harry."

"That'll be the day. Imagine him telling Barry Koontz—"

"Forget it, Rosie. Harry's never had any manners when it comes to you. I don't know why. He was probably jealous because you've always been my best friend. Anyway, what do you care about what Harry said? It was just macho boy talk."

I couldn't tell her why I cared. I wanted to. But it was just too humiliating. For all the trite stories about a best friend falling for a gorgeous older brother, I couldn't really let Jeanie know my feelings. Did Harry like me or not? I was really afraid to find out. Every boy was supposed to like me.

"Right," I said, in total disagreement with her.

"So tell me this. Why are you going out with your *mother*?"

"I can't tell you, Jeanie."

"You can't tell *me*?"

Of course I could tell her. "It's confidential, so don't tell anyone. So listen—some guy asked her out on a date."

"Your mother?"

"My mother."

"Mothers don't date, Rosie."

"Grow *up*, Jeanie."

"Can you imagine *my* mother dating?"

"Your mother has your father. My mother has no one."

"She has you."

"I know it. And she needs me. She actually came to me for advice. Can you believe it? That's why we're having dinner tonight. So I can give her my advice."

"And what are you going to tell her, Rosie?"

" 'Go for it, Mom!' That's what I'm going to tell her. 'Go for it, Mom!' "

"Go for what, Rosie?"

"That's *exactly* what I'm going to find out."

9

"Boy, am I glad I have a date with you instead of with the guy I had a date with," I said to my mother when we'd sat down in Trattoria Freddy. "He was really obnoxious when I cancelled our date. You saved me from an evening of exquisite torture. Believe me, Mom, there's nothing worse than a date with a guy you don't even know."

"But isn't that what dating's all about? Meeting new people and getting to know them? I mean, when you go out with people you've been going out with for a long time, like your fiancé or your husband, you don't call it dating, do you?"

"Mom, I didn't even know this guy's name."

"You had a date with a boy whose name you didn't even know? What were you going to call him? Supposing you got trapped in an elevator and you had to call to him for help? What would you scream? 'Help me, date. My date, my date, help me, help me.'"

"Very funny, Mom."

She laughed. "I thought so myself."

"Speaking of names . . ." A man's voice startled both of us. "I couldn't help overhearing you two fine young ladies, and I wanted to introduce myself. My name is Carlo. I am your waiter. I am here to serve you and to make your meal a memorable one. Can I get you beautiful ladies a cocktail before I tell you our specials and I leave you alone for a few minutes to contemplate our magnificent menu?"

"What do you think?" asked my mother. "Rosie, what do you think about a *drink*?"

"For *me*?"

"Of course not. You're too young. For *me*."

"Ladies?" said the waiter, who was getting impatient.

"You're old enough to decide for yourself," I said to my mother.

"Of course I am. But I feel I'm putting myself in your hands completely tonight. That's what's so special about this. I mean, you *are* taking me out to dinner. You *did* cancel another date for me. I never *was* very good at picking a drink, even when I was young and dating your dad. I never knew the difference between a Bloody Mary and a Screwdriver and a Rusty Nail and a Sidecar and a Bullshot and a—"

"Ladies!"

"A glass of white wine for my mother," I said, "and a Virgin Mary for me."

"Ah," said Carlo loudly, as if he were announcing our order to the entire restaurant, "*vino bianco* and a Virgin. A fine choice. On the rocks for that Virgin?"

"Thank you, no," I said just as loudly. "No rocks for this virgin."

"Rosie!" said my mother.

"*Dio mio!*" said Carlo, who almost ran to get away from us.

"Rosie, is this what you're like on dates? So brash? So outspoken? I mean, what must the boys think of you?"

"I don't give them a chance to think."

"I'll bet you don't."

"Besides, they never get a chance to tell me. I never go out with the same guy twice."

"You don't? What's the matter? You can't find anyone you like?"

"That's part of it."

"What's the other part?"

"The other part, Mom, is that no one asks me out for a second date."

My mother reached out and took my hand. It was one of those automatic gestures that came with being a mother. You think your kid is confessing some unhappiness and *zap!* your hand shoots out and grabs her hand. I knew a lot of people my age would rather be caught dead than be found sitting in a restaurant with their mother holding their hand. But not me. I loved my mother. I always had. And I loved her even more now that she needed me so much to help in her new life as a Dating Mother.

"You poor thing," she said.

"Mom," I explained, "I haven't met a guy I'd *want* to go out with a second time. If I did, I'd make sure he asked me."

"How would you do that?"

"Uh-uh," I said. "None of my dating secrets until you tell me some of your own. Now who is this guy? What's the story here? What's going on with you? How come you didn't accept? And why did you tell him that you'd have to discuss it with me first? Come on, Mom, level with me. I can't help you out until I know the whole story."

"You really want the whole story?"

"Of course I do."

But before she could begin, Carlo swept up to us with a tiny tray held aloft in one hand over his shoulder.

"Ladies, your drinks have arrived! *Vino bianco* for the lovely lady. A Virgin Mary for the young lady with the fiery eyes. *Salud*, ladies, *salud*. And now"—he whipped a notepad out from some pocket he seemed to have inside his shirt—"our specials!"

For the next ten minutes Carlo interrupted the most important conversation between me and my mother to recite a list of special soups and salads and pastas and fish and chicken and grilled meats. Each one he described in detail, not only what was in it but how it was cooked. His face lit up with each new dish. His mouth more than watered, it bubbled. His eyes grew as each dish was seasoned, then narrowed to slits as he served it, in his imagination. He made everything sound wonderful. He made me want to order one of each. That's when I knew he was a great waiter.

"Carlo," I said.

"Ah, my name."

"We are in your hands. Serve us whatever you think we will love."

I thought he was going to twirl his tray on one finger. "*Signorina*, you do me a great honor."

I smiled at him. "And now we are going to talk so . . ."

"But of course. But of course. Carlo will leave you now. But he will return with the greatest meal you have ever eaten. I can assure you, ladies, you will *never* forget your meal from your waiter Carlo at Trattoria Freddy tonight."

"So long as it's not from the garlic alone, Carlo," I said.

"Ah, garlic," he said, kissing his palm as he ran toward the kitchen.

My mother was in shock. "You're letting the waiter order all of our food?"

"That's how it's done sometimes, Mom."

"How did you get to be so sophisticated, Rosie?"

"I read books. I see movies. And I've been out on so many dates I just am, Mom . . ." Then, while we sipped our drinks, I regaled my mother with stories I had never told her before—stories of some of my more amazing dates.

10

"Ladies," Carlo said with a flourish, doing a half-twirl of the large tray over his head before bringing it down to his waist and placing it on one of those folding tray-hammocks. "I have here for you, specially chosen at your request by Carlo, two absolutely marvelous antipasti. For you, my dear lady," he said to my mother, drawing close to her ear, "I have *Ostriche al Pesto*, which is oysters, cooked in the shell with pesto, which of course is a base of basil mixed with olive oil, what else?, and safflower oil and a little walnut and parsley and some nice pepper for a little spice. Very good. And for you, precious young lady, I have a cold antipasto, which is called *Insalata di Fagiolini e Calamari*, which of course is a salad of green beans and squid. I know you like squid. What not to like? I swear to you, this squid will make your teeth dance. And now, *buono gusto*, dear ladies. I will leave you in peace to enjoy your meal. More wine for the lady? Another Virgin Mary for *la princessa*?"

"*La princessa?*" I said. "Since when did I get to be *la princessa*?"

"You eat the squid," said Carlo, "you are *la princessa* in my book. So, more drinks?"

"Sure," said my mother.

"Thanks, Carlo," I said, as he went away happy.

"Whew," said my mother, "he sure comes on strong."

"He liked us," I said.

"Are you sure, Rosie? I mean, what sort of person would bring people squid when they hadn't even asked for it?"

"But Mom, I love squid."

"You do? But how . . . I've never cooked squid in my life. I've never even tasted it."

"Mom, when you've been out to as many restaurants with as many guys as I have, you end up trying *everything* after a while. Sometimes you order strange things just to keep awake. I mean, some guys are so boring that only the prospect of something like eel in aspic is enough to keep you from falling asleep over your Tab. Would you like to try some squid?"

"Some squid?" She sat way back in her seat.

"Go ahead, Mom."

I stabbed a piece of squid on my fork and leaned across the table. My mother closed her eyes and opened her mouth. But I could tell she was also clenching her nose from inside.

It took a while for her to close her mouth around the thing. Finally she bit down on it, once, twice, and then over and over again. "It's chewy," she announced. "It doesn't have any taste, thank goodness. But it's chewy. I kind of like it. It's like gum that you've been chewing for a day or two. Maybe a week." She laughed. "Squid. I can't believe it. I'm eating squid. I swear, Rosie, having a daughter these days is like having a mother."

What a nice thing for her to say, I thought. How was I to know how screwy things were going to get?

"An oyster?" she offered me.

"No, thanks." I mean, how could I possibly confess to her that the thought of eating an oyster made me want to barf? Oysters? Please! Cooked or raw, they were disgusting. You might as well order an antipasto of sneeze.

11

"So who is this guy?" I asked, getting back to the important subject of the evening.

She took another mouthful of oyster. She wasn't ready for another mouthful of oyster, but she took it. Just to keep from having to answer my question.

"Is he cute?" I asked.

My mother swallowed. "Cute? What kind of a question is that? Cute? I don't know if he's cute. I don't even care if he's cute. Cute? Rosie, he's a grown man. Grown men who are cute look ridiculous."

"So is he handsome?"

"Handsome?" She put her hands over her face. I think she was straining to see him in her mind, or else she had a tiny picture of him embedded in her palm. "Of course he's handsome!" she exclaimed. "He's gorgeous. I swear it to you, Rosie, this man is the best looking man I've ever laid eyes on, let alone spoken to. Even if all I did say to him was that I'd have to ask my daughter if I should go out on a date with him. Gee, what a coward I am. But maybe he's *too* good-looking for me. What do you think, Rosie? Maybe I should set my sights on a man who looks more like . . . I don't know. More like the kind of man who no one ever notices except the woman who's in love with him, and she thinks he's the handsomest man who ever walked the earth, because he *is*, to her. So what do you think?"

What did I think about *what*? My mother was going on like a teenager. I decided to play it cool and just ask the questions. "Well, is he nice, Mom?"

"Nice? Is he nice?" There she went, back to her palms again. "I'd have to say he's about the nicest man I've ever met. But he's not just nice, he's *wonderful*. He has great manners and a soft, strong voice, and he's polite and kind and gentle and considerate and generous and . . . well, yes, I'd have to say he's nice. What do you think?"

What did I think? The guy sounded like a saint. "He sounds nice to me, too. Really nice. But let me ask you a question."

"I wish you would," said my mother, putting another oyster into her mouth. "Your questions are really helping."

"You seem to know this man pretty well, Mom. It sounds as if maybe you're already dating him. And you don't really need me to tell you what to do at all. So just how long have you known him? I'd really like to know."

"How long have I known him?" said my mother. "May I try your cold green beans?" And before I could accuse her of stalling, she had her fork into my food and was lifting it to her mouth.

"How long, Mom?"

"An hour," she said.

"What?"

"Maybe closer to forty-five minutes. Look, I've finished all your food *and* mine. I must be hungrier than I thought."

"Forty-five minutes? You're as bad as I am, Mom. Forty-five *minutes*?"

"And luckily for us, here comes Carlo."

Like clockwork, there came Carlo. He put his tray down on the stand and snapped his fingers over his shoulders. Two busboys came running toward us from opposite ends of the room and took away our plates.

And that's when Carlo served us the main course.

12

My mother had *bistecca alla diavola*, which was steak in a hot pepper sauce. Carlo said it was just right for her because she looked like "a little devil" herself, "if you don't mind if I whisper that in your pretty ear, *contessa*," he screamed loudly enough for everyone in the restaurant to hear.

Me he gave *pollatini di petto di pollo e maiele*, which sounded like some kind of game you played with your pets, especially the way Carlo announced it, but was really just chicken rolled up with pork stuffing in the middle.

After Carlo had moved his hands over our plates several times and described every ingredient in both dishes, he waltzed away like a toreador and I said to my mother, "He's flirting with you."

"He is not."

"He called you a little devil."

"I know. Why do you suppose he did that?"

"He likes you."

"So he called me a little devil?"

"He thinks you're hot, Mom. Just like your steak. That's what *alla diavola* means. He did it on purpose. He ordered you hot stuff because he thinks *you're* hot stuff."

My mother got a whole new look on her face. She beamed. She looked the way I hadn't seen her look since I was a little kid, and she and my dad would hold me between them, with their arms interlocked around me, and he would look at her and she would look at him, and I would look at them. She would be beaming. Dad too. But now I remembered my mom, and I could see her then, as now, looking like she loved herself because she loved us.

"Well maybe I am," she said. "Maybe I am hot stuff."

She laughed. Then we both ate for a while, not saying anything, enjoying our food and the silent company of one another.

Finally, when we were both done eating, I said, "So this man is the handsomest man you've ever laid eyes on and the nicest man you've ever met. And you've known him for a total of maybe an hour, max. So who is he, Mom? Just what's going on here?"

"Okay," she said. "I'll tell you. But first let's have some coffee. Some espresso." She put her right hand into the air, snapped her fingers, and called, "Carlo, oh Carlo. The *contessa* is calling you, Carlo." And then my mother just about collapsed in laughter.

"This is the most fun I've had in years," she said.

"I'm so glad to hear that, madam," said Carlo, who was directing an army of busboys who were clearing our places completely—dinner plates, bread plates, cutlery, glasses, dirty napkins, everything.

"Oh, I'm so sorry, Carlo. But I was talking to my daughter."

I thought that would hurt Carlo's feelings. But Carlo

was Mr. Perfection. "Your daughter? I cannot believe she is your daughter. Your sister, maybe. But your daughter? No! I refuse to believe it. You are too young. You are too beautiful. You are too . . . slim. And so for dessert we have—"

"*Due espresso*," said my mother.

"No dessert?" said Carlo. "No rum cake, no *zabaglione*, no *gelato*, no *spuna di cioccolato*, no—"

"No," said my mother. "Just *due espresso*."

"No fruit? No cheese? No—"

"Dear Carlo," interrupted my mother. "Please leave my daughter and me alone so we can discuss my love life."

"Your . . . what?"

"My love life."

"Truly?" Carlo seemed genuinely astonished.

"Yes." My mother nodded.

"But I would truly like to listen," he said.

"Just bring us two espressos," my mother commanded. Off he went.

"And your love life," I reminded her.

But my mother only shook her head. "I was just showing off. What I said before is true. I've known him only an hour. Maybe less. He came into our office looking for a house to rent. He's a visiting professor at Plainview College. He's going to be here only next semester. Then he's going back."

"To where?" I asked.

My mother looked shocked. "My goodness. I have no idea. I don't even know where he comes from. What if he comes from someplace like New York City? I wouldn't even know what to say to someone from New York City. I mean, what if he's so sophisticated that he eats sushi for breakfast and he whistles classical music in his sleep? Really, Rosie, this man is already three steps ahead of me and miles over my head."

"Mom," I said sternly, because I hated to see her lose

her confidence before she'd even gotten it, "he's not from New York. New Yorkers never come to Plainview. He's not from New York. And besides, even if he is, who cares? He's here now. He's here for a whole semester. He asked you out on a date. A date takes only an evening. Not a whole semester."

My mother slapped her hand into mine. "Well, I know that, silly. But one date does lead to another."

"Not for me it doesn't. I haven't been out more than once with any guy since . . . since . . . since Gary Howell tricked me into a second date with him by calling me up and changing his voice and pretending he was a guy named Hitch Mitchell and asking me out. So of course I went."

"Who's Hitch Mitchell?" asked my mother.

"That's just it, Mom. He didn't exist. Gary Howell just made him up. Just to get another date with me."

"You mean you accepted a date with this Hitch Mitchell and you didn't even know who he was?"

"Sure. Why not? Anyway, who could resist a date with somebody named Hitch Mitchell? He sounds like an absolute idiot."

My mother held up her hands. "Now wait a minute. You're telling me you accepted a date with a person who doesn't even exist."

"Right," I said proudly. After all, how many other girls could make that claim?

"And secondly, you accepted the date with this nonexistent person because you thought his name made him sound like an idiot?"

"Of course," I said.

"But *why*?" asked my mother.

"Because I didn't know it was really Gary Howell," I explained.

I thought my mother was going to go crazy there for a second. She slammed her hand down on the table. Fortunately there was nothing on it but an empty ashtray. "No, no, no, no, no. I mean, why would you date someone just because you thought his name made him sound like an idiot?"

"Oh," I said, now that I understood. "Well, if he *wasn't* an idiot, there was only one way to go, and that's up. And if he was, so what else is new?"

"Is that why you date so many boys, Rosie? God, that's a question I've been meaning to ask you for years. Is it because they disappoint you?"

I nodded. But I said, "Mom, I prefer to look at it this way—even though I admit that almost every guy *is* an idiot, no matter what his name is. But I prefer to look at it like this—I'm in a search for perfection. That's all. I want the perfect guy. And the only way to know if a guy is perfect is to date him. Right? So what about you and this college teacher? Are you going to go out with him or are you going to chicken out and turn the poor man down?"

"That's where you come in," she said.

"Well, you've asked me, Mom. And I've listened to you. And I've given this a lot of thought. And I say, Go for it, Mom. Go out with the guy."

My mother leaned way back in her seat. That's when I realized that my role in her love life was not yet played out. "I'm happy to have your encouragement, Rosie. I really am. And I'm glad you feel I should date him. But there's one more thing I really need from you before I can accept."

I braced myself for this one. "What's that, Mom?"

"I want you to meet him."

"What? Me? But I—"

"You see, Rosie. I didn't tell you the entire truth. I not only told him that I had to ask you if I should go out with him. I also told him I'd have to have you meet him. So say you will, Rosie. It'll be fun, I promise."

She wanted me to audition this man for a date. What a great idea! Maybe I could put Jeanie to the same use for all my dates. My mother had just created a whole new profession: the Date Evaluator.

"But what if I don't like him, Mom?" I said, to give her a way out.

"Oh, you will," she said. "Professor Fuller—that's his name, by the way, Rosie—Professor Fuller is the most wonderful man in the world. Next to you, of course," she said to Carlo, who stood there serving us our espressos.

"You flatter me, madam," he said. I thought he was going to leap into her arms.

"I know I do," said my mother. "But isn't it just so much fun?"

All three of us laughed at that.

It was wonderful to see my mother come alive again, after all her heartache over her divorce. And it was wonderful to be such a big part of it.

I couldn't wait to meet the new man in her life.

"Check, please," I said to Carlo.

I loved the way he looked at me when I said that.

I felt I was the real woman in the family now.

13

Before I could deal with my mother's love life, I had to deal with my own.

I wasn't getting anywhere. I'd had too many dates and too little fun. I hardly knew who I was. I hardly knew who the boys were. They were a succession of phantoms. They were boys to look at beside me as if they were mirrors and I'd be able to see myself in them. But I never did. I was looking in the wrong place. Those boys were like all the crazy things people bought at La Maison de Trash. They were only as useful as people imagined them to be. And they were no longer useful to me. They weren't Harry. They weren't going to help me get Harry. And I wasn't only leading *them* on by dating them. I was leading *myself* on. To where? To the maison de trash that my own silly life had become.

It was time to break free of the tyranny of perpetual dating.

So I called Jack Trumbull.

"Jack," I said, "I can't see *Top Gun* with you on Saturday."

"Why not?"

"Because I've got another date."

"Another date? Who with?"

"Professor Fuller."

"Who?"

"Professor Fuller," I repeated.

"What is he, a teacher?"

"At the college," I explained.

"You're going out with some old fogey instead of me?"

"That's right, Jack."

"I'd like to shoot him right out of the sky," Jack said. Then he hung up on me, thank goodness.

I told the same thing to Paul ("Bruce") Ashworth, Steve Pease, Allan Filbert, Arnie Bullock, and Jeff Keisling. And to Ron Falsey, Gene Stemkowski, Bull Francis, Lester Cousins, and to the other guys on the football team, whom I hadn't told Harry Higgins about because he hadn't given me a chance. Of course, I had told him that I was just kidding about those guys. But I hadn't been. I was date crazy.

But not anymore. Now all I cared about was my date with my mom and Professor Fuller.

But I couldn't go on calling him Professor Fuller. None of my ex-dates understood. They all thought I'd thrown them over for someone who was so old I wasn't even allowed to know his full name.

"Mom," I asked her when I got off the phone after breaking the last of my dates for the next month, "what's Professor Fuller's first name?"

She put down her book. "You know, Rosie, that's a very good question. When we met, I introduced myself as Mrs. Dupuy, and he introduced himself as Professor Fuller. And that was that. But it's funny you should ask, because I was wondering the same thing myself. 'What *is* that man's name?' I ask myself. But of course I don't have the faintest idea."

"Mom, you're almost as bad as I am."

Because she loved me, she smiled at me. "Why is that, Rosie?"

"Because sometimes I don't know the names of the guys I date either."

Now she pushed her book aside and held open her arms for me. "Like daughter, like mother," she said, as she gave me a hug and hung onto me as if she really believed that the secrets of love could be passed from one body to another.

"I'm so nervous about our date with Professor Fuller," she said.

I patted her on the back. "Don't worry. With me along, you have a hundred years of experience in a sixteen-year-old body."

"But what if you don't like him?" she asked.

"The story of my life," I said. "But there's always someone else. Remember that, Mom. For every guy you meet, there are approximately a hundred million guys you haven't met. And that's in the U.S. alone."

"Oh, but I do hope you like this one."

"For his sake," I said, "so do I. Because he's getting the best woman in the world. Even if she doesn't know his name."

She shook her head, let go of me, and bent down for her book. "Oh, I'm so silly. Can you imagine going through life calling someone 'Professor Fuller'?"

"Forget about going through life. Let's just hope we get through Saturday night."

"Do you think he'll call soon?"

"They always do."

And of course I was right. I was always right when it came to men.

14

When the phone rang with that fateful call later that very same night, I let it ring long enough for my mother to answer it.

I was doing homework in the den, where my father used to do all the work he brought home from his office when he still lived with us. But now it was mine. After he moved out, my mother could never stand it when I disappeared upstairs (on those rare evenings when I didn't have a date) and closed the door to my bedroom to do my studying.

I couldn't stand it either. Even my own room was more lonely with my father gone.

So without either me or my mother suggesting it, I had started to study in the den. It made her feel someone was there for her. And it made me feel someone was there for me, even if it was only half of my parents.

The phone was in the living room, which was between

the den and the kitchen. Once it had rung long enough, I went to get it.

And there was my mother, standing right next to it, staring down at it, with her hands folded over the bottom of her face.

"Go ahead, Mom," I urged her.

Her eyes pleaded with me. I didn't know what it felt like to be this nervous about some boy calling you, but I knew that if somebody didn't answer the phone, he might never call back. I know I didn't call back certain guys if they didn't have the sense to pick up the phone when I felt like talking to them. Which was practically never, anyway.

"Hello," I said.

"Mrs. Dupuy? This is Professor Fuller, and—"

"This is *Ms.* Dupuy," I said.

"Oh, I'm terribly sorry. I thought it was Mrs. Dupuy, Ms. Dupuy. Well, anyway, this is Professor Fuller, and if you'll recall you were going to do me the honor of allowing me to take you and your daughter out to—"

"This *is* my daughter," I said, before I realized what I was saying. "I mean, this is *her* daughter. I mean, she's my—"

"Mrs. Dupuy?" he said. I could tell he was really confused.

"Yes," I answered.

"This is Professor Fuller," he began again. "Do you know who I am?"

"Sure I do."

"Oh, thank goodness. For a minute there . . . anyway, when we met the other day, and I asked you if you would like to see me on Saturday night, and you said—"

"I said I would have to ask my daughter," I said. I mean, if this guy didn't know the difference between *Ms.* Dupuy and *Mrs.* Dupuy—between me and my mother—then I'd do my mother the favor of being her with him.

"Exactly," he replied. "And then you said—"

"I said that I would like her to meet you."

"Precisely." He sounded very pleased to think we were on the same wavelength. "Well, Mrs. . . . I mean, Ms. Dupuy, I'm calling now to confirm the date we made for the three of us to get together."

"Great," I said. "I can't wait to see you again. . . . What did you say your first name is, Professor Fuller?"

"Oh, I didn't say. But I'd be happy to now. Shall I?"

"Sure. Go for it, Professor."

"Go for it . . . ? You certainly sound different than you did the other day, Ms. Dupuy. You sound much more *spirited*, if you don't mind my saying so. The other day you were a trifle . . . reserved . . . even nervous."

"Me? Reserved? Nervous? Excited, maybe. But nervous, never."

"Excited? About what?"

"About meeting you, Professor."

"Meeting me? Oh, how kind of you to—"

"About selling you a house, Professor."

"Oh, not selling, my dear Ms. Depuy. Rent to me, yes. Sell to me, no. As you'll recall, I'm here for only—"

"—one semester. Yes, I remember, Professor. But once you get to know me a little better, you're going to want to stay here in Plainview for the rest of your life."

It was around this time that my mother started to panic. She had one hand over one ear, as if that would keep her from hearing how I was setting this guy up for the best date he'd ever had in his life. And had the other hand over her mouth, as if she could keep me from talking by gagging herself.

Professor Fuller laughed cautiously at what I'd just said. "You have an ingenious way of trying to sell homes, Ms. Dupuy. Very effective. Very *flattering*. But I can assure you I've got a wonderful apartment back in New York, and I have no intention of—"

"You're from New York City?" I shouted.

"Oh, no!" my mother screamed.

"Yes, I'm from New York," Professor Fuller said calmly. "Wonderful city. And I hope you'll pardon my asking, but who was that screaming in the background there? I quite distinctly heard—"

"Oh, that's just my daughter," I said.

Now my mother put both hands over her mouth. It was better than if she'd put them over her ears, because it was important for her to be able to listen to how a pro handled a guy on the phone.

"Does she always scream?" he asked.

"Only when she's about to meet a very handsome, very wonderful man."

"Is your daughter going out on a date tonight? Isn't it rather late for her to be—"

"I'm talking about *you*, Professor."

"Me? Handsome? Wonderful? Ms. Dupuy, are you still trying to sell me a house?"

"Of course I am, Professor. That's my job. And you have to expect a woman to do her job. And do it right. Right?"

"Of course," he answered. "But—"

"—but it's also the truth. You *are* handsome. You *are* wonderful. And my daughter and I are so looking forward to our date with you. But there are two questions I have to ask you."

"Of course."

"What time are you going to pick us up on Saturday night?"

"At seven o'clock."

"Make that seven-thirty," I told him. I knew you've always got to get any date started on *your* terms, not the guy's.

"Of course. Seven-thirty it will be. And your other question?"

"What's your first *name*, Professor Fuller?"

"Oh, yes, I did promise to tell you. Well, here it is. My name is . . . now don't laugh at me, Ms. Dupuy. My name is . . . Stanislaus. Please don't laugh at—"

It was too late. I was laughing. I guess that was the difference between being sixteen, like me, and being almost thirty-seven, like my mother. Someone sixteen is still young enough to laugh at someone's name. But a person who's almost thirty-seven . . .

Through my laughter, I whispered to my mother, "His name's Stanislaus."

"Oh, God, no!" said my mother. She started to laugh so quickly that she was standing next to me one second and the next second she was bent over holding her stomach and checking out the shine on her shoes.

"I *knew* you would laugh," said Professor Fuller. But the good part about it was, he was laughing too. That was when I realized I might be able to actually like this guy.

"How about I call you Stan?" I asked him.

"Nobody ever has," he said.

"See you Saturday, Stan."

15

Jeanie let me work at La Maison de Trash on Friday night. I had to make some money. That great dinner with my mother had practically cleaned me out.

I was selling a man a watch that ran backward while I told Jeanie all about our big date the next night.

"It's really the most exciting thing," I said. "I mean, teenage dating just pales next to this. This is the real thing, Jeanie! My mother is almost thirty-seven years old. And this Professor Stanislaus Fuller sounds like he's about the same age going on a hundred. He talks like a real professor. He's very formal. But I can tell that deep down he thinks my mother is the greatest thing since CDs. And *I'm* the one who's going to decide if he's right for her. *Me.* 'Dear Rosie' —maybe I can get a dating-service column in the *Plainview News*. I could pick the right men for the right girls. I could even *date* all the men ahead of time."

"You already have," Jeanie cracked.

We both laughed and gave each other a high ten.

"So how do you tell time with this thing if it runs backward?" said my customer.

But all I wanted to do was talk to Jeanie, so I ignored him and said to her, "Yeah, I know I have. But listen to this. I called up all my dates and I broke them. Jack and Steve Pease and Arnie and Allan and the football team and—"

"But why?" Jeanie was obviously shocked. Not that she'd ever really approved of the indiscriminate way I tried to put a little excitement into my lonely life. But she'd certainly been impressed by my ability to get dates out of thin air (which pretty much describes the insides of the heads of the guys I'd been dating).

"So tell me this," said my customer. "Is it that a watch that runs backward is more accurate than a watch that runs the regular way?"

"All those guys just don't mean anything anymore," I told Jeanie. "I'm sick of dating one guy after another and never the same guy twice. I can see from watching my mother that a lot is at stake. This date with Professor Fuller is the most important thing in her life. And for me, a date has always been just a nothing. And the more dates I had, the more nothing they've become. *That's* why I sometimes don't even know the names of the guys I go out with. I was just trying to get out of the house, Jeanie. And that's no excuse for a date. What I'm looking for now is a date that's the most important thing in *my* life."

"It may be a little late for that, Rosie, I hate to tell you. You may be all dated out by now."

"So tell me something else," said my customer. "Can it make you dizzy, telling time on a watch that runs backward?"

"That's my fear, too," I confessed to Jeanie. "My dating days may be over. No guy may ever mean enough to me to make me want to date him. And so all I'll have to look forward to in life is checking out whether my mother's dates are right for her."

"What a grim prospect," said Jeanie. "I mean, I can't quite imagine going through life as my mother's chaperone. Of course, I can't quite imagine my mother dating. Right, Mom?" she hollered over at Mrs. Higgins.

"Right, Jeanie," Mrs. Higgins shouted back. That was her theory of raising her two kids: they were right about everything. Except, of course, for Harry. There was something wrong with Harry, and it was this: Harry was too good-looking. This created lots of problems for him. For example, he was so much in demand that he made no demands of his own. He could go through life never having to say hello to anyone who didn't say hello to him first. That's the problem with good looks. They can make life so easy that love ends up hard. Hard to show and hard to feel, even if it's not hard to find. That was Harry. You could love him, but he'd never love back.

"So what's the big deal about this watch?" asked my customer.

"I'll tell you what's the big deal about this watch, sir," I said. "The reason this watch goes backward is so it can make you younger. For every hour it goes backward, it makes you an hour younger. For every day, a day younger. For every year, a year younger."

"Is that true?" the man asked. That's when I knew I had a sale.

"Sure. Look at me. I'm my own mother's age. But I don't look it, do I?"

"You certainly don't," he said. "But—"

"Why, tomorrow night, my mother and I are going out on a date with the same man. And *he* thinks I'm *her*."

The man's hand went into his pocket. He was mine. "You mean he thinks you're your own mother? A young-looking lady like you?"

"That's right," I said.

"Gimme two of those watches," he said.

"Good idea, sir. One for each wrist, right?"

"Heck, no, lady. You don't think I want to get young all that fast, do you? Next thing I'd know I'd be wearing short pants and playing a kazoo in mud puddles. No, I want to give one to my wife. She's old now, but she's still beautiful. And all I want to do is see her again the way she was when she was your age. That's when I met her. And I forgot to look at her back then. I mean really look at her, memorize her. So I want to go back in time. Do you think this watch will really help us—me and my wife, I mean, not you, you're too young to want to get anywhere but older—do you think it will help me and my beautiful wife to go back in time?"

"Of course it will," I said. Not that I believed it. But I wanted it to, for this nice man's sake. And for his beautiful wife's. What he really wanted was to be where I was now, me and Harry, Jeanie and whoever her first love might turn out to be. These were the most precious moments of our lives— that's what he was trying to tell us. And he was willing to buy two backward watches just to prove it.

"I knew it!" he said. "So gimme two. You know, you're the best darned salesperson I've *ever* seen, girl. A backward watch." He winked at me. And I knew he knew it was all an illusion, a beautiful illusion. "I'll bet you could sell rust to a body shop."

"What a great idea," said Jeanie. "Instant rust. I'll bet we could sell cans of it."

"G'bye, girls. Wait'll I give this backward watch to my wife. We can both wear them and watch ourselves get younger. But we'll never be as young as you two ever again. That was a once-in-a-lifetime experience. Don't waste it on the wrong fellas."

The man took off across the mall with a skip in his step. It must have been because he was wearing one of the watches I'd sold him.

"That's the first backward watch we've *ever* sold," said Jeanie, hugging me. "Until now, no one could ever figure out what they do. You're a genius, Rosie. If you ever decide you really want a job . . ."

So we were hugging like two long-lost friends when a voice said, "So what happened on your date with Barry Koontz?"

16

It was Harry. He was looking better than ever. He must
have spent all his La Maison de Trash money on the coolest
sweatshirts ever to hug the male torso and on secret facial
treatments for his great skin and invisible eyeliner for his
shocking dark eyes that shone so bright I could never look
into them without feeling my own eyes catch on fire. He
made me feel so unwanted and inexperienced. Me! The
tri-state dating champ!

"It was great," I answered. "Barry Koontz is the greatest."

Harry scoffed. "Barry Koontz is the worst. He's got a
brain the size of a grape and a head the size of a beach ball.
The guy can't talk. He can't dance. He can hardly walk
because his thighs rub together. And his mother has to dress
him. He's just one more loser like all the other losers you
keep wasting your time with. You're out of your mind to go
out with him, Rosie."

"So why did you tell him he was out of his mind to go out with *me*?"

Harry looked around like some voice had just come out of the firmament.

"Who told you I told him that? Did he tell you I told him that? That'd be just like him, I swear it. Telling you I told him—"

"It was me," Jeanie confessed. "I told her."

"You?" said Harry. "Why did—"

"Forget *who* told me," I said. "*Why* did you tell *him* that, Harry? That wasn't a nice thing to say, you know." I meant it. It was a terrible thing to say. He thought Barry Koontz was nothing more than a dead branch on the tree of life, and he was *still* crazy to go out with me.

"I'll tell you why I told him that," said Harry. "I'll tell you." He looked at me like he was about to pronounce me the most ridiculous date a boy could have in his entire high school career. His face came so close to mine that its warmth washed over my skin, his eyes grew big enough to engulf my sight of his frightful good looks, and his hands rose toward my neck, so I thought he was going to strangle me even before he insulted me with his explanation of why I was, as far as he was concerned, unfit for the most undateworthy guy in all of Plainview.

Fortunately, we were saved by the arrival of an even worse specimen of human boydom. If he could be called that.

"Hi. Have you decided if you want to go out with me yet?"

It was the potato.

"What are *you*?" Harry asked.

"I'm a potato. What did you think I was, a bowl of chili?" The potato looked Harry up and down. "And what are you?"

I wondered just what Harry would say. A boy? A man? A model? An Adonis? An insulter of women and girls? A dream and a nightmare come true?

But the potato didn't let him answer. "No, let me guess. You're a clerk. I can see you're a clerk. You're behind the counter of the famous La Maison de Trash. So you must work here. And what else. You're a heartbreaker. I can tell that, just from the look in your eyes. Girls love you, and you look at them with those eyes of yours, and their hearts break. You don't even have to say a word to them, you don't have to tell them you're too busy to read the poems they've written to you or to listen to the songs they've composed about you. Yes, you're a clerk and a heartbreaker. No question about it. And you're also this girl's boyfriend."

The potato pointed his potato mitten right at Jeanie. "Yes, I can tell there's something special between you. *She's* not afraid of you. She's the only one who's ever been able to tame your wild heart. And I just wish I'd known that before I humiliated myself by asking you out," he said to Jeanie. "Have you ever seen a potato cry? It's not a pretty sight. Do you know what a potato cries? Not tears. *Dirt.* Is La Maison de Trash ready for a little sad dirt from the eyes of a forlorn and disappointed potato?" He put his mitten up to the eye holes in his potato head.

"Harry, tell him the truth," said Jeanie.

"Okay," said Harry. "I'm not a clerk. I *own* this place . . . sort of. And I'm not a heartbreaker. If anything—"

Jeanie punched him on the arm. "Not about *you*, Harry. Tell him the truth about us."

"Oh, my God," said the potato. "You're married?"

"Tell him, Harry."

"She's my sister," Harry said. "And I can't believe I'm—"

"Your sister!" The potato actually jumped off the floor. "Have you ever seen—"

"I can't believe I'm talking to a potato," Harry went on.

"Have you ever seen a potato cry tears of joy?" the potato went on. "It's not tears. And it's not dirt, either. It's . . . a sour cream and applesauce–stuffed potato skin!" And with that, he produced the potato skin in its little cardboard box and handed it to Jeanie.

"You remembered!" she said.

"Everything about you," he said.

"What's going on here?" asked Harry.

"Nothing much," answered the potato. "Except I'm trying to get your sister to go out on a date with me. Who knows, maybe you and I will be brothers-in-law one day, Harry. Maybe you can even be best potato at our wedding."

"Do you realize this potato just asked you to marry him?" Harry said to Jeanie.

"Hey, folks," said the potato. "Let's not jump to conclusions here. I didn't ask her to marry me. You ought to know better than that. A potato would never ask a girl to marry him before the first date. I mean, let's take this one step at a time. All I want now is a date. Okay? A date. What about it, Jeanie?"

"Are you going to go out with this potato?" Harry asked Jeanie.

"I didn't say I was," she said.

"See," Harry said to the potato.

The potato put his mitten over the place on his potato skin where his heart would be.

"But I didn't say I wasn't," Jeanie added.

"See," the potato said to Harry.

"My sister's not going out with a potato. Who are you, anyway? Take that thing off so we can see if you're even human."

I wanted to say to Harry, And you take yours off so we can see if *you're* even human.

The potato shrugged. "Sorry. What you see is what you get," he said, which was just what he'd told me and Jeanie when we'd asked him the same thing back at the Potato Man stand. "So what do you say?" he asked Jeanie. "Will you go out with me?"

"I don't know," she said. "I don't date."

"And you think I do?" said the potato.

"What's your name, anyway?" Harry asked him.

"Call me Spud," said the potato.

That did it. We *all* broke up laughing. Even Harry, who tried not to because he was working so hard to protect his sister's honor. But even when his face was scrunched up trying not to laugh, it was beautiful. And when Harry let the laughter out, the whole mall lit up, just like when the clouds part over the skylights and the sun shines in on all the happy shoppers.

17

Jeanie walked Spud back to the Potato Man stand. It wasn't a date exactly, but it was the most alone I'd ever known her to be with any guy, no matter how he was dressed.

Harry and I watched them as they walked away from us. They turned toward Potato Man at the corner where Aw, Sheets, the linen store, meets Each Sold Separately, the toy store, and we couldn't see them any longer.

I realized then that I was alone, for the first time in my life, with Harry Higgins.

I didn't know what to say. I knew what I wanted to say. But I didn't know how to say it. I wanted to say, "You stuck-up fool. Standing right next to you is the most sophisticated, most experienced, sharpest, funniest, maybe not the prettiest—although some people think so—but deep down inside nicest, and to be perfectly honest maybe the loneliest girl in Plainview. And you don't even notice me, you skunk!"

Instead I said, "He's not bad, for a potato."

"It's embarrassing," he replied.

"Oh, he doesn't seem to mind. In fact, I get the feeling he *likes* dressing up that way."

"Embarrassing for *me*." Harry put his finger to his chest, in exactly the same place I wanted to lay my head. "Jeanie's my sister. I can't have her running around with a guy dressed as a potato. How do you think that makes me look?"

I was afraid to say. The way he looked was not something I felt comfortable talking to him about. I'd never been good praising boys. I'd always been afraid that they would take it personally. So I decided the best thing would be to do the opposite. "Is that all you can think about? Yourself?"

"Look who's talking."

"What's that supposed to mean?"

"You're as bad as I am," Harry said.

It was the story of my love life that that was the most honest thing he'd ever said to me.

"Can I help you?" Harry asked.

Oh, yes, you can help me, Harry.

Except he wasn't talking to me. He was talking to a customer, who just happened to be a teenage girl who said, "Do you have any love potions?"

"Sure we do," said Harry, who was always at his liveliest when he was selling something to someone. "What kind?"

"What kinds are there?" asked the girl. She was giving Harry the once-over, but Harry didn't seem to care, thank goodness. He looked at her the same way he looked at me: not as a girl but as a kind of stop sign he'd come upon as he was traveling the road of his life. He stopped because he had to, but he wouldn't stay.

"Well," he answered, "we have love potions for a man to give to a woman to make the woman fall in love with him. We have love potions for a man to give to himself to make him fall in love with a woman. We have love potions for a woman to give to a man to make him fall in love with her. We have love potions for a woman to give to herself to make her fall in love with a man. We have love potions for a man to give to a woman to make her fall out of love with him. We have love potions for a man to give to himself to make him fall out of love with a woman. We have love potions for a woman to give to a man to make him fall out of love with her. We have love potions for a woman to give to herself to make her fall out of love with a man. In addition, we have love potions for a man to give to another man so the second man will fall out of love with the woman that the first man is in love with. And of course we have love potions that a woman can give to another woman so the second woman will fall out of love with the man that the first woman is in love with. Also, we have love potions that a man can give to another man so the second man *will* fall in love with a woman that the first man used to be in love with but now he wants the second man to fall in love with her so the first man can fall in love with someone else, and he can give that second woman one of the love potions I told you about before, to make her fall in love with him. And of course there's a love potion for that first woman of the first man to make *her* fall in love with the second man, and I recommend that in that situation you should buy both love potions because it isn't going to do any good for the second man to fall in love with the first woman if the first woman is still in love with the first man, especially if the first man has already given a love potion to the second woman, because then he'll have both women in love with him and he'll only be in love with the second woman, and the second man will only be in love with the first woman, who's still in love with the first man, which means that nobody's going to end up very happy. So what do you say?"

"What do I say?" said the girl. She was standing there looking at Harry with glazed eyes. "It sounds terrible. It sounds worse than high school."

"Well, this'll make it better," said Harry. "That'll be one of each then?" he asked. He bent and from beneath the counter brought up a huge box filled with little stoppered glass vials filled with love potions in all different colors.

"One of each!" screamed the girl. "I only want one. I only wanted one in the first place."

"Fine," said Harry. "Which one?"

"The one to make *you* fall in love with *me*," said the girl. I thought she was going to reach over the counter and grab Harry by the hair when she said it.

"Oh," said Harry. "We're out of stock on that one."

The girl seemed very sad all of a sudden. "Well, I'll give you a deposit for when you get it in. But you have to promise to drink it."

She handed Harry a five-dollar bill, but he gave it back to her. "Sure I'll drink it," he said. "But I have to tell you something. And I think it's going to make you change your mind."

"Nothing could make me change my mind. My name's Samantha, by the way. I'm in your homeroom."

"Nice to meet you, Samantha," Harry said.

"You never noticed me before?" She looked pained. "I mean, I only sit two seats away from you in homeroom."

Harry shook his head. "As I was saying, I have something I think you should hear before—"

"Order me *two* of those love potions—if you promise to take them. You really need them."

"But that's just it," said Harry. "You see, Samantha. I'm immune. I always have been and I always will be."

"What?"

"That's right. So many girls have come by here and bought so much of this love potion and made me drink it, that I'm immune. It's terrible, I admit it. But I'm immune to it. And I'm immune to girls. But here, try this one." He handed her a vial filled with a black liquid.

"What does this one do?"

"This one is for the woman to take to make her fall out of love with the man."

The poor girl looked at it as if it could cure her whole life. "Okay, I'll take it."

"And you might want to follow it with this one," said Harry, holding up a light brown love potion and then slipping it into the girl's hand like the great salesman he was. "This is the one my sister takes."

"Your sister? And what does this one do for you?"

"This one," said Harry, "makes you fall in love with a potato."

"With a what?" Samantha was looking at Harry as if she'd never seen him before.

"A potato," he repeated.

She slammed both of the vials down on the counter. "You're terrible. I hate you."

Harry picked up the black love potion and looked at it. "Did you drink any of this?" he asked Samantha.

"Of course I didn't."

"I think you did. Because it worked, didn't it? A minute ago you were in love with me. Now you hate me. That's what love potions do. They're magic. Just like human life. I mean, you never know from one moment to the next just who you're going to love and who you're going to hate and who's going to love you and who's going to hate you."

"Well, there's one thing I know," said Samantha defiantly.

"What's that?"

"I wouldn't fall in love with a potato if it were the last man on earth. Or you either. Good-bye." She turned on her heels and walked away.

"Wait, Samantha. Perhaps I can interest you in our special corn on the cob dental floss . . ."

But she was gone.

Harry was starting to put away the love potions when I said, "You were terrible to her."

"I know."

"So why?"

"I'm not like you," Harry said. "I don't lead people on. I don't go out on date after date. If it isn't going to work out with someone, I don't pretend it is. I just stop it. Like that." He snapped his fingers.

Well, so did I. Why else had I had more first dates and fewer second dates than anyone in history? Harry and I were just alike—both of us waiting for perfection. Except I'd found mine. He was perfect for me. So what if he was vain—and sometimes cruel? Even his faults were perfect. They were a lot like mine. With our good looks united we'd be an excellent team. We'd look like a commercial for designer clothes. We'd be perfect.

"But isn't it sad?" Harry asked.

I thought he was referring to poor Samantha. But he wasn't. He was referring to the love potions. "Isn't it sad that these things don't work?"

18

That's the way I felt the next night when I was getting ready for our big date with Professor Stanislaus Fuller.

If only I could give a love potion to the professor to make him fall in love with my mother. If only I could give my mother a love potion to make her fall in love with the professor. Life would be so easy.

Or maybe I was just a control freak. Because I really enjoyed this. I liked telling my mother what to wear. I liked reassuring her that everything was going to be all right and she wasn't going to make a fool of herself in front of Professor Fuller.

"Is dating always this hard?" my mom asked me when we were at the most difficult part of any date—waiting for the guy to pick us up.

"You get used to it," I said.

Truer words were never spoken.

Professor Fuller showed up at our door carrying a beautiful bouquet of red roses.

"For you," he said, "dear Mrs. Dupuy." And he laid those flowers ever so gently across my mother's surprised arms.

"And for you, young Ms. Dupuy," he said, giving me a huge wink. And from behind his back he produced a single red rose and put it right between my fingers.

He wasn't at all what I'd expected. Not that he was as handsome as my mother had said. And to tell the truth, I hadn't expected much, seeing as how my mother hadn't really looked at any guys for years. I had thought he was going to be one of those dried-up old professors with stooped shoulders and tiny little eyes that never had any life in them except when he announced a surprise quiz.

But Professor Fuller was a great big guy, not fat but big and round and tall, with long hair in the back and huge tortoiseshell glasses and big laughing eyes that made you smile just to look into them.

"Why, these are so lovely, Professor Fuller," said my mother, hugging her roses. "I just don't know what to say."

But I did. "Thanks for the flower, Stan."

"Stan," he said. "Stan. It *was* you, wasn't it?"

"What was me?"

"It was you on the phone the other night. Pretending to be your mother."

"Of course it was me," I said proudly. "You don't think I would have let you talk to my mother before I checked you out myself, do you?"

"Of course I don't," he said. "I could ask for nothing finer than to pass muster in the eyes of so discerning a young lady as yourself."

"Why, thank you," I said. And then I made a little joke. "And I certainly hope we can pass the mustard to you."

Professor Fuller laughed and clapped his hands together and said, " 'Pass the mustard!' Oh, I do like that. 'Pass the mustard.' You're a regular little wordsmith. There's nothing I like so much as a bit of word-play. Particularly at awkward moments like these, when we've only just met and there's so much ice to be broken and you can't imagine how to begin—you're frozen yourself." He chuckled. "So tell me, Ms. Dupuy. What's *your* name?"

"Rosie," I said.

He clapped his hands again. "Oh, Rosie, Rose Rose Rosie, I just knew I'd brought the right flowers!"

The rest of the evening got even better.

Stan drove us way beyond the Plainview city limits, into the countryside, to a beautiful stone restaurant at the bottom of a hill.

We got out of the car and stood beneath the moonlight. There was the sound of rushing water from nearby.

"It's beautiful here," my mother said. "I've lived in Plainview all my life and I've never even seen this place. How did you find it?"

"I just pointed my car and drove toward paradise," he said.

I thought my mother was going to melt right there in the parking lot. "What's the name of this place?" she asked.

I could sense Stan's smile in the semi-darkness. He chuckled as he said, "Come over here. Read this."

We went over to a small plaque on the side of the building.

"Depuy Canal House," my mother read. "I don't believe it."

"It's not spelled the same way as your name. But otherwise, it's you! Let's go in." And he held out his arms so each of us could take one.

It was a very old place, with wide-planked floors that tilted first one way and then another. We were shown to a room on the second floor with only four round tables in it.

We took the table nearest the fireplace. We were bathed in its light. I had never seen my mother look so beautiful.

Stan indicated that I should sit between him and my mother. I felt like a queen. Or maybe a chaperon.

Because I was between them, I could see everything that passed between them—and everything that passed between them passed through me. I felt I was in control of everything —my mother's life, Professor Fuller's life, and my own happiness. For once, I wasn't thinking about boys and how they always let me down. For once, I was out on a date and I wasn't suffering any disappointment.

Stan took charge of the whole meal. He ordered glasses of champagne for himself and my mother, and Poland Spring water for me.

"It's a seven-course meal here," he explained, "and we're having all of them."

The food was incredible. We shared things like scrod and spinach gnocchi in dried red tomato for our soup course and black trumpet chanterelles for an appetizer and beef tenderloin in an oyster sauce and port wine for a main course. Between the appetizer and the main course we all had fennel sorbet to clear our palates. It was like eating ice cream in the middle of a meal, except it was so ultra-sophisticated I wished the whole world could have seen me eating there in that little ancient room with the great Professor Fuller and my lovely mother.

With the main course, he ordered a bottle of red wine so old that not only wasn't I born when it was made but my mother said she'd been in the second grade. "Let us hope the wine has aged as beautifully as you have, Mrs. Dupuy," said Stan, as he held his glass aloft and then touched hers with it.

"You can call her Ellen," I said.

"Ellen," he whispered like a secret between them.

As if it were my reward, he let me taste the wine from his glass. I was prepared to keep from making a face, but when I tasted the wine, I thought I'd swallowed sunlight. I could feel my cheeks turn warm and the insides of my eyes burst open. I couldn't see the future but I could feel it. There would be contentment forever.

When we were done eating—and we ate every bite of our seven courses, including our dessert of chocolate soufflé with French yellow cream—Stan told us about himself.

"I've lived in New York City all my life," he said. "I know most people think New York is dirty, noisy, crowded, and rude. And maybe it is sometimes. But to me it's the city of dreams, full of the most interesting people in the world and the grandest buildings and the finest paintings, which can transport you to every civilization that has ever existed. To live in New York is to be able to escape from your life at any moment you choose. Because New York contains the rest of the world and you need only step out of your narrow mind in order to step into another, glorious life."

"Then what are you doing in Plainview?" I asked.

"What a good question." He looked at me in a way that made me feel I'd finally found someone who knew how smart I really was. "I came here because I was lonely. Oh, I have many friends in New York. They will be waiting for me when I return, and they will be my friends forever. But I noticed that I was getting tired of myself when I was with them. Because the other thing New York can be is a small town. I didn't quite know who I was any longer. And I got lonely—not because there weren't other people around but because there were too many other people. I started to feel lost among them. Lost and lonely. So I applied for a short-term job in the English Department at Plainview College. And it was my good fortune that a professor there was taking a sabbatical for a semester. So here I am! And it was my very good fortune that in looking for a nice house to rent to make my stay here as comfortable as possible, who should I meet but the beautiful Mrs. Dupuy."

He raised his wine glass at my mother.

She raised her wine glass at him.

"To your happiness," I toasted both of them with my own wine glass filled with water from the perfect north.

"Does this mean I've passed your audition?" Stan asked. He was looking at me as if his whole life hung in the balance.

"Yes, it does."

"Oh, Rosie," said my mother. She reached over to hug me.

Professor Stanislaus Fuller looked on as if we were his very own.

19

Later that night, after Stan had dropped us off, I was lying in bed trying to think about boys, except I just couldn't think of any boys to think about. It was crazy. I knew more boys than any girl in the history of western civilization, and as I tried to bring them up into my mind so I could see them and hear their voices and check out their walks and judge their clothes and look into their shifty eyes, they just kept falling back into the black unknown, like ducks in a screwed-up shooting gallery. The only guy I could make out even remotely was Harry Higgins, and he would only say bad things about me. "You're vain, Rosie. You're cruel, Rosie. You don't know what you really want, Rosie." "I want you," I said. "I'm immune," he said. "But so am I!" I screamed, "I'm immune to everybody but you." "Me too," he said, and I was happy in dreamland until he added, "I'm immune to everybody but myself."

How could he not want to love me? Didn't he see how I was suffering for him, even in my dreams?

"Go away," I said, because I was afraid to say, "Come here."

He obeyed me instantly. He was gone, and in his place was Professor Stanislaus Fuller.

It was amazing. There I was, lying in my bed in the Plainview High varsity sweatshirt that one quarterback or another had given to me, conjuring up the image of a rather large, rather old, rather wonderful college English teacher, who seemed to be just as crazy about my mother as she was about him.

And I was jealous! Not that I wanted to start dating Stanislaus Fuller myself. But I wanted to be like my mother all of a sudden.

It looked so easy. She meets a guy, and he asks her out, and she goes out with him, and they have a wonderful time, and he drops her off, and he shakes hands with her (he's so courteous I just want to hug him!), and he says, "I'll hope to see you again soon, Ellen," and my mother doesn't even have to say anything, she just smiles at him, and he says, "Oh, good. Good," and he starts to whistle as he walks to his car in the glorious moonlight and I could swear he even skips when he reaches the end of our front walk.

I thought life was supposed to get harder as you got older. But it certainly looked like dating got a whole lot easier. And the guys were a whole lot nicer.

I was thinking about how nice my mother's new boyfriend was, when there was a knock on my door.

For a moment I dreamed it was a completely new guy I'd never met and he'd heard I was having trouble finding boys to fill my mind, which of course was the only way I could ever get to sleep, counting boys instead of counting sheep, and he'd come to my door in order to rescue me from emptiness by jumping into my mind so there would be at least *someone* I could have for company in my terrible loneliness, when the door opened and there was my mother.

There was my mother, still in the clothes I'd helped her pick out for her date and the makeup she'd kept checking with me before her date, and with a big smile on her face to replace the terrible look of worry she'd worn just a few hours before when she hadn't known just what was going to happen when she brought her daughter along to audition the first man she was going to date since before that daughter had even been born. Incredible!

"Oh, I'm so glad you're still awake," she said. She came over to my bed. "May I sit down?"

My mother hadn't come into my room at night since I was a little girl who was afraid to get up in the darkness to get my own glass of water.

I patted the bed next to where I lay.

"What have you been doing, Mom? How come you're still dressed? How come you haven't taken off your makeup? Did you forget how?"

She laughed. "I don't know what I've been doing. I've just been sitting. I feel so wonderful, Rosie. It was such a wonderful evening. You were so wonderful. He's such a wonderful man."

"How wonderful," I said. But she didn't even notice my slightly sarcastic tone.

"I know. Isn't it wonderful!" She reached down and took me in her arms and hugged me to her. "It was paradise. That's what it was. Just as Stan said. He pointed the car and drove toward paradise. Isn't he wonderful?"

"Yes," I said, because it was true.

"You know, Rosie. I think that was the best date in my life. Not that I've had all that many. I mean, I dated your father before we got married. And those were great dates, too. Don't get me wrong. But I was different then. I wasn't a woman yet. And I didn't know how hard it can be for men and women to get along. But once you know things like that, you can appreciate it all the more when the right man comes along. Really, that was the best date in my whole life. And I owe it all to you." She stroked my forehead. Maybe I was still her little girl. "But you haven't told me, Rosie. What did *you* think?"

"It was the best date in my whole life too," I said, and for some unknown reason, I burst into tears.

My mom's reaction was terrific. She held me and told me how wonderful I was and how much help I'd been and how if it hadn't been for me, she would never have gone out with Stan in the first place.

"So I suppose you're going to dump me now that the two of you hit it off so well," I said, once I'd finished crying and my mother was done praising me to the skies.

"Are you kidding? You're my lucky charm. I want you along. I know that sounds weird. But we're a family—you and I. There's me, and there's you. And if a man wants me, he gets you. So he'd better be prepared to have you along."

She didn't seem to be just saying it. I could see the relief in her eyes. My poor mother was still an amateur at the complicated game of love. So she wanted a tried-and-true pro along with her. And that was fine with me. But how come she was so good at it all of a sudden, and I was such a failure?

I guess it didn't come down to how good you were at dating.

Everything depended on who you dated in the first place. And in that, my mother was way ahead of me.

She had Stan.

From my string of boys I was down to zero. I had nobody.

"It's a deal," I said. "He gets me."

20

I rushed to the mall the next afternoon to tell Jeanie about my date with my mother's date. But Jeanie didn't seem all that interested.

Why should she be? Jeanie, who had never had a real date in her whole life, had made a date with Spud, the potato.

"He asked me out for Friday night. After we both get off from work, of course. He said he wants to go dancing at Club Mall."

"Did you accept?" I asked.

"Provisionally," she answered.

"Oh, no." My suspicions were immediately aroused.

"Please, Rosie," Jeanie pleaded. "This is the first real date of my life. You've got to come with me. You're my best friend. That's what best friends are for."

"What's what best friends are for?"

"To help out with boys. To check them out. To provide an objective view in case the mind of the girl who's dating is totally distorted by the guy she has a date with."

"My mind would be distorted too if I had a date with a guy who dresses like a potato." I knew I shouldn't have said it. But who could resist!

"That's *not* what I meant." Jeanie bent down and reached beneath the counter and came back with a huge box filled with license plates with first names on them. "Want to help me alphabetize these?"

"Heck, no. There must be a thousand of them in there."

"More." Jeanie pointed to the side of the box. "Twelve gross," she read. "That's one thousand seven hundred twenty-eight, to be exact."

"No way," I said.

"Then at least help me look to see if his name is here."

"Whose name?"

"Spud's."

I banged my hand down on the box. "You think they have the name Spud on one of these license plates?"

"Sure. Why not? You should see some of the names they put on these things, Rosie. We sell them to people who have names like Godiva and Chlorine and Cinderella and Porky and Spear and Jump Shot and Piggy Sue and—"

"You mean Peggy Sue."

"No, I mean *Piggy* Sue. And Zit and Melony—spelled like a melon, you know, and . . . well, you don't think La Maison de Trash just sells a bunch of license plates that say Robbie and Jennifer and Jason, do you? Not on your life. We have twelve gross of miniature license plates with the weirdest, strangest names ever to be given to human beings. And *that's* why I think Spud's in here. So help me find it, okay?"

I looked down at that box filled with almost two thousand license plates. I shook my head.

I could tell from the look on Jeanie's face that she'd been bluffing anyway. That was her way of negotiating with me. Get me to say no to helping her find Spud among the Wildebeests and the Jockstraps and the Sighonaras and all the other crazy names people took for themselves, and I'd be sure to say yes to acting as a chaperon on her first date with Mr. Missing License Plate, Spud . . . or her first date with anyone, for that matter.

"Listen, Jeanie," I said. "You know I love you and you're my best friend in the world and everything. And I'd lay down my life for you if a speeding train were coming our way and I had to sacrifice my own body to save yours or if there was a poison potion that one of us had to drink to save the other one, you know I'd claw your eyes out to get at that drink before you got to it. But I *don't* want to help you with the hopeless task of trying to find Spud's name on a license plate, and even if it is there, I don't care, because what is the earthly use of a tiny license plate that says *Spud* on it, anyway? What is this guy's real name? And what does he look like under that potato outfit? I mean, can you answer those questions for me?"

"No, I can't," she admitted. "But I don't know him that well yet, Rosie. That's one of the reasons I want you to come along on this date with me. What if he turns out to be a total slobola? And what if I don't even recognize that fact and I'm sitting there gazing dreamily into the eyes of a guy who couldn't even be sold as an irregular in a closeout shop."

"But how is he so far?" I asked.

She took one of her hands off the license plates and put it onto one of mine. "As a potato, he's a knockout. He's the nicest guy I've ever talked to in my life. He's funny and charming, and he seems to like me so much it's almost embarrassing."

"It *is* embarrassing, Jeanie. The guy is always dressed as a potato. But aside from that, you don't need me at all. He's crazy about you. It's obvious from everything you say."

"Rosie, so far the *potato's* crazy about me. I don't even know the guy. Maybe the guy *hates* me. Maybe he can only like girls so long as he's a potato. Maybe when he takes off his potato suit, and he's a guy, all he'll like is potatoes. I mean, why else would a guy take a job in Potato Man? Maybe potatoes are his life, his passion. Maybe he only asked me out because none of the *potatoes* will date him."

I laughed. "Jeanie, be serious."

She was flipping through the license plates like a maniac on a mission of importance only to a maniac. "I *am* being serious, Rosie. I need you to come with me. I need you to protect me."

"From *what*? From a guy? Guys are guys, Jeanie. The basic thing to know about guys is that they're more nervous about girls than girls are nervous about them. I know that sounds impossible. But it's true—take it from someone who used to be nervous going out with guys, until I took a real look at the guys going out with me. They try to hold your hand—and what do they try to hold it with? Wet palms, jumpy fingers, a grip like a dead person either with rigor mortis or with no bones in his hand at all. They try to talk to you—trembly voices, clearing their throats, cracking like sopranos or like someone goosed them. They can hardly walk—their feet keep getting tangled up. They don't know which side of you to walk on, so they keep crashing into you, switching from one side to the other. They try to give you a present, and they don't know what to say—so they shove it in your face and say, 'Here.' They don't really even know how to dance, so they make up these dances and they look like rubber puppets. It's so embarrassing to be seen with guys sometimes, I'm telling you! They order something for you in a restaurant, and they're so scared of the waiter that they treat him like he's one of their teachers. And then they finally take you home from your great date and they try to kiss you and even if you let them their lips are like caterpillars that have attached themselves to their faces and now are trying to attach themselves to *your* face. They squirm, they wiggle, and all of a sudden they seem to die for a minute and they just lie there pressed dead and hard against your own lips until they turn into the whale that swallowed Jonah, if you know the story I'm referring to, and they try to swallow your entire mouth. And why, Jeanie? Why are boys *like this*? I'll tell you why. Because they're nervous, that's why. They don't know girls. They don't know girls at all. And they know they don't. So that makes them all the more nervous. And that's what makes boys such easy dates and such terrible dates at the same time. They're easy because you can make them do anything you want to, once you realize how nervous they are. And they're terrible because they *will* do anything you want them to, and pretty soon you get tired of guys like that and you just stop going out with them. Like me. I've stopped going out with them. I've stopped dating completely. But look at it this way—you're getting all the benefit of my great expertise. Believe me, the potato is as nervous as you are. *More.* So remember that and have a good time."

Jeanie finally stopped tossing the license plates around, looked at me, and said, "Are you saying you won't go out with me and Spud on Friday night?"

"Yes," I finally admitted. "That's what I'm saying."

"But why, Rosie? Why?"

"Because I'm sick of being a chaperon. At least I think I am. I mean, it's one thing to go out with my mother and Stan, who at least wasn't nervous and who I liked a lot, I have to admit it. Too bad he's old enough to be so old. But I can't go out with you and Spud. It would be embarrassing for all of us. You need to work all these things out yourself. You're my best friend. And I wish you and Spud all the best. But no. I will not escort you on your date or run interference for you on your date or tell you at the end of your date whether you ought to marry Spud or to bake him. And that's all there is to it. My answer is no."

I thought Jeanie might freak out, but she just nodded at

me and went back to fingering her way through the license plates. "Well," she said, "I *was* hoping for a second opinion. Now the only person I'm going to be able to depend on is Harry."

"What do you mean, Harry?"

"Harry said he'd come to protect me. But protection is one thing. Helping me figure out what I feel about Spud is another. I can't trust Harry to—"

I couldn't believe it. "You mean Harry's going on your date with you?"

"Don't look so shocked, Rosie. He doesn't have anything better to do Friday night, except work here. And Mom said we could both leave early. But now he probably won't want to go. I mean, who's Harry going to dance with while I'm dancing with Spud?" she asked.

"Me," I answered.

21

On Friday night I picked up Jeanie and Harry at La Maison de Trash.

Mrs. Higgins seemed delighted at seeing all of us together, dressed up specially and ready to step out for a night on the town.

"I just wish *your* date were here," she said to Jeanie. "Then I'd take a picture of you with my Nimslo camera. It takes three-dimensional photos, you know."

"Well, we have to pick him up at work," Jeanie explained.

Mrs. Higgins nodded. "I hope to meet him before too long. Not that I want to meddle in your life, Jeanie, my dear. But this *is* your first date. It's certainly worth capturing on film. And in my memory." She touched her head.

Mr. Higgins peeked around from behind a counter, where he'd been dividing a shipment of David Lee Roth dolls into those with clothed behinds and those with bare behinds.

He was throwing out all the bare behinds. He always said that La Maison de Trash had standards to maintain.

"Jeanie, don't listen to your mother," he said. "She doesn't want to memorize your date. She wants to size him up."

"Well, maybe we'll stop by here when we're done dancing. How late are you staying open?"

"I think we'll close up at midnight tonight," Mr. Higgins said.

Plainview Mall was open twenty-four hours a day, every day. Not all of the shops and stores stayed open eternally, but there were always moviegoers, and hungry people, and wild young things like us, ready to dance the night away, who might drop in to shop.

"So maybe we'll see you later," Jeanie said to her parents.

"Take care of your sister," Mr. Higgins said to Harry.

Harry looked toward the skylights and shook his head.

"And you take care of Harry, Rosie," Mrs. Higgins said to me.

Harry covered his eyes.

I just hoped I'd get a chance. The only reason I was going along on this crazy date of Jeanie's was because of Harry. But why was Harry there? And was he my date? And if he was, what kind of date was this anyway? But if the only way to get close to Harry was through Jeanie and Spud, so be it. I'd chaperon them right up to their wedding in some vegetable patch.

"I do," I said to Mrs. Higgins. "I mean, I will."

Spud was waiting for us at Potato Man.

"Hey, great," he said when he saw us. "Let's go."

"Aren't you going to change, man?" Harry asked him. He was already protecting his little sister.

"Change into what?" asked Spud. "An avocado?"

"Change your *clothes*," said Harry.

"But this is me," said Spud. He turned to Jeanie. "This is the guy you accepted a date with. Mr. Spud."

"My sister isn't going out on a date with a guy dressed as a potato."

"Hey," said Spud, "I don't have anything to change *into*—I come to work dressed this way, and I leave work dressed this way. That's what's great about this place—they let you take your uniform home. They trust you. And—"

"Yeah," said Harry. "Of course they trust you. Who could possibly try to run off with a potato outfit?"

"And third of all," continued Spud, "I think you ought to let your sister make up her own mind. What do you say, Jeanie? Do you have any objection to going dancing with a guy dressed as a potato? Do you really mind going out with a fellow who it's guaranteed will be like no other fellow in all of Club Mall? Does it really bother you to be seen with a boy like me?"

"Heck, no!" said Jeanie. I could tell she really meant it. Her eyes were bright, her smile was wide and real, and her hand nearly slipped into Spud's potato mitten. That's what inexperience could do for you—you could date a guy dressed from head to toe like a potato and really be happy about it.

"Well, then, let's go," Spud said, and he took Jeanie by the arm and led the way to Club Mall.

22

Club Mall was a huge place down at one end of the mall, past the indoor Sears automotive center and the video rooms where old-fashioned-looking teenagers dressed like from the early 1980s hung out playing Laser Love, and The Stamp Collector, where strange boys went with their fathers on weekends and they always brought their own tweezers to pick up stamps, and the Mall Playhouse, where plays were put on and sometimes famous actors from TV soap operas came to act in things like *Desire Under the Elms* and *The Muppets Take Plainview*.

Club Mall was the largest structure in all of Plainview Mall. It was even bigger than the Mall Twentyplex which was twenty movie theaters in one building, was open for twenty-four hours just like the rest of the mall, and where they sold the famous Twenty-for-the-Price-of-Eighteen discount tickets, for people who wanted to see each movie and were willing to do it without leaving the premises for about two days running.

There were always at least three live bands in Club Mall, and on Friday and Saturday Funkmaster Fagin was there to create fabulous dance mixes in the main ballroom.

The place had about ten separate dance rooms, catwalk-balconies so you could take a rest and watch everybody dance from above (and see how ridiculous human teenage life could look), and low, cushioned couches in every room for various kinds of rendezvous.

There was a sign near the entrance that said: CAPACITY 10,000 PEOPLE. ANY EXCESS WILL BE IN VIOLATION OF PLAINVIEW FIRE LAWS.

So they often had to turn people away, particularly on weekends after midnight.

People came to Club Mall from the whole tri-state area. Teenagers had been seen wearing Club Mall T-shirts as far away as Los Angeles and the Comoro Islands, where a kid from Plainview High once went to join the French Foreign Legion.

One teenaged couple was found living in Club Mall. It turned out they'd been reported missing over a year earlier and had spent that entire time dancing and taking naps on the couches and sponge baths in the rest rooms and leaving Club Mall only when they felt the urge to go window shopping in the mall itself or for pizza at one of the mall's nine pizza stands. Now they were trying to get into the *Guinness Book of World Records* as the people who had lived the longest in a teenage dance club.

As for me, I'd been to Club Mall many times, with many guys. But I'd never been there with a potato. And I'd never been with Handsome Harry Higgins.

Spud took Jeanie off to dance right away. Funkmaster Fagin was way up in his booth near the domed ceiling of the grand ballroom, flashing out his famous dance mix of "Rock-a-bye Baby." It was the funkiest song imaginable.

It brought back all our childhoods but bathed them in absolute hipness.

With Jeanie and Spud gone into the crowd of dancers, I was alone with Harry.

I'd been alone with Harry before, at La Maison de Trash. But I'm not afraid to admit it—I didn't know what to do. I didn't know what to say. I hardly knew how to breathe.

No guy had ever had this effect on me before. Especially no guy I'd known since he was six and I was four. If that wasn't illegal, it should be. It wasn't just how gorgeous he was, although that had a lot to do with it. After all, looks may not be everything, and looks may not be the only thing, but they certainly are right there up front when you need them, and if the only thing you're being offered is somebody's looks, then it's looks you grab onto and hold onto, until something more important comes along. But what's more important than looks? Looks seemed safe. What you see is what you get. That's how I figured it.

Anyway, it *wasn't* just how gorgeous Harry was. I didn't want a boyfriend so handsome that every girl in town wanted to buy him a love potion. I knew there was something *else* besides looks. I didn't think guys asked me out because of my looks alone. I never really wondered why they asked me out. Could it be I had a reputation for not saying "No." Not the "No" to "doing it," just to dating. Were guys just dating me to test going out? Did guys hate someone saying no—some girl hurting their feelings? After an experience with me, was a guy ready for someone else? I didn't want to pursue these thoughts. I refocused on Harry.

Harry was the most aloof person I'd ever met. I'd known him all my life practically, and he was still the biggest mystery to me. I wanted to solve him. Somehow, I felt I would never know myself until I knew Harry. I would have been as embarrassed about Jeanie's dating Spud as Harry was. I felt more like his sister than Jeanie. I felt Harry and I were on the same wavelength. But he didn't know it. Or if he did, he didn't want it to be so. But if Harry didn't like me, I reasoned that it meant he didn't like himself. And if he didn't like himself, he'd have to be the biggest fool around. And I didn't like fools. I decided that Harry must like himself, which meant he had to like me, which meant we were made for each other, which meant our romance was safe.

But what romance?

That was the trouble with Harry. I didn't know what he wanted from me. I only hoped it was me—not just my great looks and my vast experience with lesser mortal boys than he.

I started to dance to the music. I was afraid to ask him to dance, but I thought maybe he could take a hint. You always see girls dancing alone at clubs. It's not because they want to do a Billy Idol. It's like male strutting, which we learned so much about in biology. But how come they never teach us about female strutting? Girls on parade. Looking for boys to admire us. Looking for boys who are worthy of us.

Harry didn't ask me to dance. About a dozen other guys did, but not Harry. At first I kept saying "no." Harry was just looking out over the dance floor, the chaperon supreme.

If Harry wasn't going to be with me, I felt awkward just being alone. Finally, I decided to dance with a stranger. It was the story of my life, so I might as well live it.

"Do you mind?" I asked Harry, and I nodded toward a guy dressed all in black leather with studs running up and down his sleeves and his pants legs and skull and crossbones earrings in both ears and a bandanna tied around his forehead. He was standing a foot away from me and snapping all ten fingers to the beat.

Harry looked the guy up and down. I guess the only reason he didn't close his eyes in bewilderment at my choice of a dance partner was because his own sister was out there at that very moment dancing with a potato.

"Mind?" said Harry. "Why should I mind?"

Because I want you to mind, you fool! Because I would never in a million years dance with a boy like this if I weren't doing it to get you to mind that I was doing it in the first place.

But now I had no choice. I let this pirate carry me off among the thousand teenage feet. But not so far that I couldn't keep an eye on Harry, or let Harry keep an eye on me, if only he would.

"They call me Stud," the guy said.

"I wonder why," I answered, as his entire outfit flashed in the lights stabbing the dance floor.

"Whatta they call you?" he asked.

Lonely, I almost said, but instead I shook my head and put my hands over my ears, pretending I couldn't hear him over Funkmaster Fagin's mix of New Order's "Bizarre Love Triangle."

Then I danced my heart out, just to show Harry how many moves I had and how I could dance this guy Stud into the floor.

But whenever I looked over at Harry, he wasn't looking over *at* me. He was looking *over* me.

I thought maybe he had a secret girlfriend somewhere on the dance floor. But when I followed his gaze, I saw it always landed on Jeanie. Not that I could see Jeanie. But Spud was unmistakable. His huge potato head rose out of the crowd, warts and all, bopping merrily to the beat as if all potatoes had been born to boogie.

Harry, I thought, look at me, Harry. I'm dancing for you to look at me, Harry. I'm dancing every step I know and I'm twirling around in *both* directions and I'm doing deep knee bends so I can shoot up into the air high enough for you to think you've seen a shooting star and I'm getting close enough to this guy that I'm nearly getting stabbed to death on his studs. And still you won't look at me. Harry.

"Stop dancin' like that," said Stud. "You tryin' to show me up?"

Stud was trying to keep up with me. But he couldn't.

His black leather clothes were too hot. I was melting him right down to his studs. He didn't like it.

I saw he had a red bandanna in his back pocket just like the one around his head. I plucked it out and wrapped it around my fingers and started to wipe his face with it. That made Stud smile. He grabbed my wrist and held my hand so I would keep treating him tenderly. He must have had on razor rings, because my wrist hurt. I didn't know how long I could stand it—the pain and his sweat soaking through the bandanna right onto my own skin. I didn't know how long it would take for Harry to see what this guy was doing to me and what I was doing to him.

I looked over at Harry. He wasn't hard to find, even though he was in the middle of the large group of people who ringed the dance floor, waiting for their own lives to begin. Was he looking at me? My eye caught his. It did. I know it did. I found that so hard to believe that I blinked. And when I was done with my blink, I looked again. Now Harry's eyes were on Jeanie and Spud. But hadn't they held mine, for at least a moment? Would I ever know for sure?

"What're you lookin' at?" Stud asked me when he saw me following Harry's gaze.

"Some friends of mine over there."

"Where? You got a boyfriend I don't know about?"

"Yeah," I answered. "But he's not over there. He's over there." I looked toward Harry.

"I'm your boyfriend now," said Stud, and he held my wrist even harder. "And if that guy thinks he's your boyfriend, I'm gonna soul him."

"You're gonna what?" I mimicked him in my tough-girl voice.

"Soul him. I'm gonna take his soul. I'm gonna separate his body from the rest of him. I'm gonna remove his breathin' from . . . *Ooweeee.*"

Stud started to shriek because at that moment Funkmaster Fagin segued right into Nitzer Ebb's "Murderous." It must have been Stud's theme song. He began to pound on the floor with his huge black motorcycle boots. He motioned for me to do the same.

"Let's do the Stomp!" he screamed.

It was the newest dance sensation. It was so new that Stud was making it up on the spot. And he started to Stomp his way right over toward Jeanie and Spud.

"Show me your friends," he said. "I wanna tell 'em about us."

"Tell 'em *what* about us?"

"That you're my woman, woman."

I laughed. "Yeah. Let's go tell 'em that, Stud. That I'm your woman."

So we Stomped over to where Jeanie and Spud were dancing. They had a lot more room to themselves than any other couple, because Spud's behind was so big in his potato suit. They were holding hands as they danced. Or at least Jeanie had ahold of both of Spud's mittens. She was looking up into his potato eyes. He was looking down into her human eyes. They didn't see anything else in the world, including me and Stud.

"Here they are," I said to Stud.

"Who? Where?" he panted. The Stomp wasn't a hard dance to do, but it took a lot out of you.

"Hi, Jeanie. Hi, Spud," I shouted at them over the music. They stopped dancing and finally took their eyes off one another.

Stud couldn't believe his eyes. "These freaks are your friends?"

"Sure." I introduced them. "Jeanie, Stud. Stud, Jeanie. Stud, Spud. Spud, Stud."

Spud held out a mitten to shake Stud's hand. "Isn't it nice how our names rhyme," Spud said to Stud.

"I'm Stud's woman," I said, and I gave Jeanie a great big wink.

"Stud, Spud. Spud, Stud," Spud repeated.

Jeanie winked back at me, but at the same time she pressed her mouth against my ear so I could hear her over the music and she whispered, "What are you doing with this animal, Rosie?"

I was about to confess to her that I was just using him to try to get Harry to pay attention to me. But Spud had finally gotten on Stud's nerves so much by trying to get him to say "Stud Spud Spud Stud" three times fast. Stud lost whatever cool he might have possessed and grabbed Spud around the neck.

"Shall we dance?" Spud asked him.

But Stud was really upset. "Take that stupid thing off, you vegetable. Lemme get a look at the face I'm gonna turn into mashed potato."

Spud didn't seem to mind that Stud was trying to rip his head off. "Then mash me the way I am," he said. "If you want mashed potato, you have to *begin* with a potato."

"You're a freak," Stud said. "You don't belong here. You look like a bozo. What's the matter with you, man? Take that thing off or I'm gonna take it off for you. You're bringin' this place down. Way down. We don't need your kind here. Why don't you go back into the ground where you belong? You're the ugliest thing I ever seen. I can't believe you found anybody to dance with you. You're a disgrace to the human race."

"I knew you were a poet," said Spud. "You rhyme everything. Stud, Spud. Spud, Stud. Say it fast three times. And when you're done, tell me why you're wearing all that jewelry stuck on your clothes."

That was as much as Stud could take. He reached down and started to pull a chain out of one of his huge boots. It came clanking out when Funkmaster Fagin blitzed into "Brand New Love" by Dead or Alive.

Just as Stud finished wrapping the chain around the black glove on his right hand and was about to swing the end of it around poor Spud's neck, to remove from him forever his kindly, ugly potato face, Harry came charging across the dance floor, grabbed the end of the chain, and pulled Stud toward him so their faces were together in a classic enemy's kiss.

"*You*," snarled Stud. "Whadda you think you're doin'?"

"Leave him alone," said Harry.

Stud tried to get his chain back, but he couldn't rip it out of Harry's heroic grasp. "Leave him alone? He's a freak. He's dancin' with our girls, man. The next thing you know everybody's gonna go around dressed like a potato, and all the girls'll be led down straight into the dirt, where this thing came from. So get your hands off me, man. It's our duty to soul this monster. He don't belong here. If he wants to dance, he can go dance in some potato field. Don't fight me, man. Help me get rid of him. We can do it together. What's he to you anyway? He's not even human. We human beings gotta stick together, man. Let's soul this sucker. Why're you defendin' him? What's the matter with you, man?"

Stud was getting hysterical, because he couldn't loosen Harry's grip on his chain.

But Harry was calm. "He's my sister's boyfriend."

"That's your sister?"

"That's right."

"And you let her go out with this potato puff?"

"That's right."

"And I suppose you'd let your girlfriend here go out with a potato, too?"

Uh-oh.

"Who?" asked Harry.

"Her." Stud pointed to me with his free hand. "My woman here. Except she said she's your girlfriend."

Just like that, Harry let go of Stud. "She said that?" Harry had a strange smile on his face. I couldn't tell if he was glad to hear the news, even if it wasn't real.

"I swear it," said Stud, who I could see was really afraid

of Harry. Harry was probably the first guy who'd ever stood up to Stud's clothes.

"You must be out of your mind," Harry said.

It was the same thing he'd said to Barry Koontz about wanting to go out with me—that he must be out of his mind.

I could barely say what I knew I had to say. "He's lying."

Harry seemed relieved. "You're lying," he said to Stud.

"*She's* lying," Stud said. "But I'll teach her. Because she's *my* woman."

"Welcome to the club," Harry said.

What club? There was no club. There was only Harry. Didn't he know that?

"There is no club," I said to Harry. And then, before they could see my tears, I ran away to the sound of Funkmaster Fagin's mix of Gene Loves Jezebel's "Desire."

I ran straight home to my mother.

23

I hadn't been lying. I hadn't said I was Harry's girlfriend. I'd said Harry was my boyfriend. Stud had it wrong.

But so did I. Harry wasn't my boyfriend. He didn't even want to be my boyfriend. He thought someone would have to be out of his mind to be my boyfriend, to have me as his girlfriend.

I'd gone out with a million guys. Who wouldn't have? I was lonely. My father and mother had split up when I was twelve, and that's exactly when I began my record-setting date pace. I couldn't stand to stay home every night. There used to be a man I loved around the house. But when he left, I left too. I wasn't looking for him. I was just looking for boys. For love. For the noise of people and the possibility, just the possibility, of being happy again.

But in all that time, I'd never had a boyfriend, had I? I'd

just gone out with boy after boy, hoping somebody would catch my fancy, and I could catch his.

But I was just a dater. I wasn't a steady. I wasn't a girlfriend. I wasn't anything except an experiment in my own existence.

And then I decided to stop dating altogether. When I saw my mom fall for a guy she'd only just met, and I realized that there was a guy named Harry Higgins who was the only guy I wanted to date, I said good-bye to boys and hello to heartache.

When I got home that night, I longed to tell my mother what was going on with me. But she didn't give me a chance. And I didn't want to take the risk of destroying her own happiness.

She was waiting up for me, sitting cross-legged in her nightgown in the middle of her bed.

That's all she was doing. Sitting. No book. No TV. No pictures of houses and condos spread out around her. Just sitting. Waiting for me. Dreaming her dreams.

It was as if she'd taken a vow of silence and the only thing that could break it was my appearance before her.

"Oh, Rosie. I'm so glad you're home. I've been waiting up for you. I have so much to tell you. You just aren't going to believe it. Of course it has to do with Stan. Stan called tonight. We must have been on the phone for hours. We talked about everything under the sun. Plus, I think I found him a place to live. It's a wonderful house. And it's just the perfect rental for him. The people who own it want to come back to it for Christmas—they'll be in Europe until then—and of course the semester will be over by then, so Stan can just move out and they can move back in and he won't be breaking the lease and everything will be perfect. Oh, he's so excited. I'm going to take him to see it tomorrow. And of course I expect you to come along. But the best news of all is *this*!" My mom was so excited, she started to play with the fringe of her nightgown, as if she were afraid her fingers would start dancing in thin air if she didn't keep them busy. "We have another date tomorrow night. He asked me where I wanted to go, and do you know where I told him? Trattoria Freddy! I'm learning, Rosie, I'm learning. And I couldn't do it without you. I'd be lost without you, Rosie. So." She clapped her hands. "He's picking us up at seven-thirty again. And we're going to have the most wonderful date in our lives. Even better than . . . but no, that's impossible. Just as *good* as our first date together. Or better. I don't know. All I know is that he called me up and asked me out and—"

That's when I couldn't stand it anymore. I reached out and took my mother's hands in mine and I said, "Mom, I can't go."

She shook her head at me. She kept shaking her head at me. "What do you mean, you can't go? You said you'd go. You're my lucky charm, remember, Rosie? I *need* you with me." She laughed, but it was a nervous laugh. "I mean, where would I be without you? What will I do without you?"

"You'll have a wonderful time without me."

"But you said you'd *come*, Rosie. You said we had a deal, remember? What could be more important than our being together? Why *can't* you come, Rosie?"

"Because I've got a date, Mom. I've got a date of my own. And it's time you stood on your own two feet. Like *me*."

Her hand went to her mouth. Her eyes filled with my betrayal. "A date? But you have so many dates. And I . . . with who, Rosie? Who?"

"The only boy I've ever loved."

My mother reached out her hand to keep me there, but I was gone already. I was on my way to live my lie alone in my empty room.

24

That night I counted boys instead of sheep, but I still couldn't fall asleep. And there weren't many boys to count. There was only one. And he didn't jump over a fence or come dashing toward me to take me in his arms and deliver me to the sweet oblivion of sleep. He ran away from me. And I ran after him!

Well, if that's what my dream told me to do, then that's what I was going to do.

On all my dates, all I ever really did was run away from boys. This time, I was going to run toward one.

I went to the mall very early the next morning. I left while my mother was still asleep. That way, she wouldn't be able to ask me again to go out with her and Stan to show him the house that afternoon and to eat with them at Trattoria Freddy that night.

When I got to La Maison de Trash, I was relieved to find that Harry wasn't there. Neither was Mr. Higgins.

Only Jeanie was there. And her mother.

Mrs. Higgins was selling some woman a set of irons that you put on your feet so you could skate over your clothes. It was meant for people with back problems who couldn't bend over an ironing board. It had always been a popular item at La Maison de Trash.

Jeanie was staring off into space while a customer was asking her a question.

I tapped Jeanie on the shoulder. She turned to look at me. Her eyes were filled with dreams. Dreams fulfilled.

"Rosie," she said, as if she had to recall my name from some great distance in our mutual pasts.

"Yes," I answered, reaching out and taking her hand and shaking it hard. "Rosie Dupuy. So how was your date last night?"

"Dreamy."

"No kidding."

"But what happened to you last night?" Jeanie asked me, finally coming out of her reverie.

"That's what I have to talk to you about. But first you ought to take care of this woman."

"What woman?"

"Me!" said the woman. "Your customer. *Me.*"

Jeanie shook her head to try to clear away whatever cobwebs love had spun there the night before. "Oh, may I help you?" she asked the woman.

That's when I knew I'd better take over. I stepped to the counter right in front of the woman and sold her the nostril-beautification kit she was holding.

"Wow," said Jeanie.

"All in a day's work," I said.

"Rosie, you're terrific. You could sell songs to a bird, I swear it. It's no wonder all the boys like you so much. You're your own best sales job. Honestly, you're incredible. But what did you want to talk to me about? Wasn't last night just dreamy? Except why did you . . . ?"

"Can we take a walk, Jeanie?"

"Sure, Mom," she called, "I'm taking a break."

Mrs. Higgins just flicked her hand for us to go. She was too busy selling. Her customer had actually taken off her skirt and was ironing it right on the floor of the store. At least a dozen women were crowded around to watch. They all had their pocketbooks open and their purses in their hands. Mrs. Higgins knew that the women of Plainview couldn't wait to step into Leg Irons.

I led Jeanie past all our favorite stores and into a part of the mall where we wouldn't have any distractions. I made her follow me into the Shopper's Chapel. Its official name was Our Lady of the Mall, so it was Catholic, but people of all religions used it, and sometimes there was even a rabbi there to assist Father Gratitus in the services. The place was always filled with people, most of them on their knees, praying for things they couldn't have, things they couldn't afford, or things they couldn't find any place for in their houses.

"What are we doing in here?" Jeanie whispered. "I haven't been here since my mother made me come after that man threatened to sue us when his Chattering Teeth started up in the middle of the night and bit his wife's nose."

I laughed. "I remember that. But we're here because I need to talk to you, Jeanie. I wanted someplace quiet. And I didn't want anybody to see us."

"You didn't want anybody to see us! Look at all the people in here. You'd think they were going back to Sunday closings and the whole world was asking God to keep the stores open."

"But it's quiet in here. And we can sit down. And I can make my confession."

"Your confession!" Jeanie took my hand and pulled me into a pew. We sat down. She didn't let go of my hand. "Your confession? You? You mean you have something to tell me that you haven't told me before? I don't know whether to feel good or bad about that. But what is it, Rosie? What? Quick. I can't stand the suspense."

She held my hand, and I held hers. "I'm in love with your brother."

Jeanie instantly threw her arms around me. "Oh, Rosie," she cried.

"Oh, Jeanie," I cried back, because I was so glad she understood and was happy for me.

"Oh, Rosie, you poor thing," she wailed.

"Oh, Jeanie," I wailed back, because I was so sad she understood how terrible it was to be in love with Handsome Harry Higgins.

Jeanie held me at arm's length and looked into my face. "He's immune, you know. That's what Harry always says. He's immune. He's never had a girlfriend in his life. He's never had a *date* in his life. Last night was the closest thing he ever had to a date, and it was with *you*, Rosie. But first you started to dance with that refugee from *Mad Max*, that Stud, and then you ran away from all of us. Why did you do that?"

"Because Harry wasn't paying any attention to me. And Stud lied to him about my being his girlfriend. I didn't say I was his girlfriend. I said he was my boyfriend."

"But he's not your boyfriend, Rosie."

"Maybe to him he's not. But to me he is. I mean, he's the only boy in my heart. Doesn't that make him my boyfriend? He's the only boy I want to be with. He's the only boy I dream about. Doesn't that make him my boyfriend? He doesn't have to *be* my boyfriend in order to be my boyfriend. I can make him my boyfriend. But I know I won't be his girlfriend until he makes me his girlfriend. And then we'll be each other's friend. But, Jeanie, I don't know how to make that happen. Do you?"

"No," she said. "Harry's strange. The only girls he seems comfortable talking to are the ones who shop at La Maison. Especially the ones who want to buy love potions.

Then he goes into that long speech of his about which love potion is for what. But by the time he's done with that, the girl he's talking to always has a glazed look in her eyes, and she'd do anything Harry wanted, absolutely *anything*. But he never seems to want anything from them. He just likes to make that speech to them because he thinks it demonstrates how impossible love really is."

"He's right on that score," I said.

"But love *isn't* impossible," said Jeanie. "I used to think it was. But look at me now."

"You're in love with a guy who thinks he's a potato."

"And *you're* in love with a guy who says he's immune to love. Me, I'll take a loving, giving potato any day."

"Does Harry really think love is impossible?"

"I suppose he does, since he's never felt it."

"And is he really immune?"

"I suppose he is, since he's never been in love. Of course, no one's ever been in love with him, until you."

"What about all those girls who come into the store and practically remove their skin for him?"

"They're not in love with *Harry*. They're just in love with his *looks*."

"But Jeanie, Harry *is* his looks."

"Oh, and I suppose you're going to tell me Spud is his looks too."

"Absolutely. I mean, no one said it was fair, but how you look is *you*. That's what's walking around in the world. Not that your looks make you a good person or a bad person. But they are the most important thing about a person when it comes to other people. Looks are what people respond to. Looks are the first thing anyone sees about you, by definition. And let's face it, looks are exciting. I mean, the thing I love most about Harry is the way he looks."

"So that's what you see in Harry." From the way Jeanie said it, I couldn't tell if she was asking me a question or telling me that Harry's looks were what I saw in Harry.

"What's what I see in Harry?"

"His looks."

"Of course that's what I see in Harry. What else is there?"

Jeanie thought for a moment. "I hate to say it, because he's my brother and I love him, but I don't know if there is anything else."

"There isn't!" I said triumphantly.

"I guess you're right. Of course, he's a good salesman, and he wears the coolest clothes, and . . ." That was about it. Jeanie stopped.

"He's cute," I said.

"I guess you're right about that."

"And I love his face."

"He does have a nice face."

"And what a bod!"

"Oh, sure." Jeanie looked embarrassed.

"So what else does a girl need?"

"But you make him sound so *shallow*."

"He *is* shallow, Jeanie. That's okay. I don't mind. You know what they say—shallow waters run cute."

"*Who* says that?"

"Shallow girls do. Like me. I'm shallow too. I know it. But I don't mind. To me it's a compliment. Life is short, Jeanie, and short means shallow. I don't need deep conversations. I don't need profound thoughts. I don't need meaningful meetings. I like simple things. I like handsome boys. That's what I like. That's what pleases me. That's what fills me with admiration for the world. Handsome boys. I mean, what else is there when you get right down to it? What else is there worthy of a girl's own love? The love of a handsome boy, that's what. Really."

Jeanie looked at me strangely. Then she broke into a big smile. "You know, Rosie. You and Harry are even more perfect for one another than I would ever have imagined. I mean, you two are just made for each other. And I know this: if the two of you can ever get together, you're going to make each other very happy. You and I will be best friends forever because we'll never want the same guy. We want very different things. But you and Harry, what a match!"

"But how am I going to get to him, Jeanie? How am I going to get a chance to make him happy?"

"You know when Harry's happy, Rosie? When he's at the store. When he's standing there letting his gorgeous looks attract people to La Maison de Trash and then he sells them pieces of marvelous junk. That's when Harry is happy."

"Then that's what I want to do," I said.

"What?"

"I want to sell some marvelous junk. I want a job, Jeanie. I want to try to capture my beast in his natural habitat. I want a job at La Maison de Trash."

"And that way . . ." she said, a smile growing on her face.

"And that way . . ." I said.

We burst out laughing. People started to shush us.

"I guess we better say a prayer," Jeanie said. "Just in case."

"Make him mine," I prayed.

"Make him hers," Jeanie said. And then she added, "And let Spud be at least as nice out of his potato suit as he is in it. Thank you for listening to our trivial pursuits, Lord."

25

"Mom," Jeanie said to Mrs. Higgins, "Rosie wants a job."

Mrs. Higgins was between customers. She was putting pictures of former-President Reagan into lockets. She looked up from her work. A picture of President Reagan stuck to her thumb and kept jumping up at me and Jeanie as Mrs. Higgins moved her hands while she spoke. "How nice. Every young person should have a job. It helps build character. It makes them aware of how hard it is to make a living. And the right job teaches them how to sell practically anything to anybody. I'm proud of you, Rosie. So where is it you want to work?"

"Here, Mom," said Jeanie.

President Reagan really started to bop around now. "Here? But Jeanie, we don't have a job *opening* here. I mean, we've never had a job opening. Don't forget, no one except our family has ever worked here. I mean, Rosie, we like you very much, and you are *like* one of the family, but—"

"Mom, that's the whole point. Rosie wants to be even *more* like one of the family."

"But you have such a nice family of your own," Mrs. Higgins said kindly. "It's a bit small for a family, I'll admit. But your mother is a very nice woman, and I know your father still loves you even if he's far away, and he *is* your father. So why do you feel you need to be a Higgins, so to speak?"

"She doesn't want to be a Higgins, Mom. She just wants to be near a Higgins."

"Who? You're her best friend already. And she's yours. So—"

"Not me, Mom. Harry."

"Harry? Oh, Harry. I see. I see." Mrs. Higgins got up off her stool and took my arms in her hands. "You want to be near Harry so he'll . . . so he'll . . . Oh, you poor thing."

"That's what *I* said," said Jeanie.

"Harry's immune, Rosie," Mrs. Higgins said. "Don't you know that? Harry's immune."

"I said that too," said Jeanie.

"Well, I'm not a disease," I said. "I'm a cure. And I'm going to make Harry healthy."

Mrs. Higgins nodded. "Well, it would be nice if *someone* could get through to Harry. I always thought it would be some new girl who came in here one day and just swept him off his feet. But maybe you're right. You've known him nearly all your life. Maybe it will take someone familiar and comfortable to make Harry sit up and realize that there's more to life than thinking the only person you can ever really love is the one you see in the mirror. It isn't going to be easy, Rosie, but I can understand why you want a job—so you can keep an eye on him, so you can be close to him. But I have only one question. Can you sell things?"

"Can she sell things!" Jeanie came to my rescue. "Are you aware of the fact that Rosie sold a backward watch? *Two* backward watches, actually. And to the *same man*."

"You did?" said Mrs. Higgins.

"And not only that," said Jeanie. "But I'll bet she can sell one of those." She pointed to the lockets. I felt my heart sink.

"Impossible," said Mrs. Higgins. "These President Reagan lockets aren't even for sale. We're *giving* them away. Or at least we're going to try to give them away. One free with any purchase. It's a *gift*, Jeanie . . . Rosie. A gift. No one could actually sell one of these things. No one."

"Rosie can," said Jeanie.

"Well," said Mrs. Higgins, "if Rosie can sell one of these, then she can certainly have a job at La Maison de Trash. But if she can't . . . well, I'm sorry, Rosie, but—"

"Don't worry," I said, picking up a bunch of lockets. "I can sell them."

"Hooray," said Jeanie, who took me by the hand and led me to the counter and to my new life as an honorary Higgins and the business colleague of Handsome Harry, the boy no girl had ever dated.

26

The problem was, I couldn't sell a President Reagan
locket. I tried person after person for my whole first hour that
morning, and everybody looked at me like I was crazy.
People who were buying pre-moistened sponges wouldn't buy
a President Reagan locket. People who were buying empty
jars of invisible ink wouldn't buy a President Reagan locket.
People who were buying joke cigars that said My Wife Just
Had a Cigar—Have a Baby, wouldn't buy a President Reagan
locket.

"What am I going to do?" I whispered desperately to
Jeanie.

"I don't know. It's impossible."

"What's the matter?" asked Mrs. Higgins.

"I can't sell a single one of these things," I confessed.

"I told you," said Mrs. Higgins. "Never underestimate
my experience in these things, Rosie. And never overesti-

mate the popularity of a former President. Especially one who spent his whole term asleep at the wheel. But I'm sorry . . . about the job, I mean."

"But Mom!" shrieked Jeanie. "It isn't fair. No one could sell a President Reagan locket. You said so yourself. And Rosie did sell a jar of invisible ink—more than a jar, actually."

Mrs. Higgins looked astonished. "You did?"

"Go ahead, tell her," Jeanie prodded me.

"Yes, I did," I told Mrs. Higgins.

"But there's nothing *in* those jars," she said.

"I know."

"So what did you do when your customer said the jars are empty?"

"I told him that nothing is invisible."

Mrs. Higgins scratched her head. "Nothing is invisible? What does that mean? We're selling *invisible* ink, after all, Rosie."

"Yes, exactly! He said there was nothing in the jar. I said nothing is invisible. And since it's invisible ink, then the nothing that's in the jar must be the ink."

"And he bought it?" she asked.

"Sure he did. Of course I told him that when he wrote his messages with the invisible ink, they would be invisible, too. He said that was fine, because that's why he was buying invisible ink in the first place. I asked him what he planned to write, and he said he was going to write a love letter to his girlfriend. I asked him why he wanted to write it in invisible ink. He said it was because he didn't have a girlfriend. 'Oh, she's invisible too,' I said. And this guy started to jump up and down, and he said, 'Finally, someone who understands me,' and then he asked me for *two* jars of invisible ink, just in case he found another nonexistent girlfriend after the first one. 'Then why don't you take them all,' I said, 'because there are millions of girls in the world, and the chances are pretty good that none of them are going to be your girlfriend.' And so he did! He bought every jar of invisible ink we have."

"He did?" Mrs. Higgins asked both of us.

"And he walked away happy," said Jeanie.

"Then you're hired!" said Mrs. Higgins, and she reached out and hugged me to her large and welcoming bosom.

27

My happiness at having a new job was cut short by the arrival of the reason I had wanted the job in the first place.

Harry came into the booth with Mr. Higgins and immediately stepped to the counter, put his hands down on it, and stuck his nose in the air.

"He's so stuck-*up*," I whispered to Jeanie.

"Oh, no," she said. "He's just sniffing for customers. That's the way he is when he gets here. He can't wait to start selling things. Harry *loves* to sell things. Sometimes I think the only time he's happy is when he's selling things. Haven't you noticed? Harry hardly ever has anything to say except to his customers."

"Yeah, he's the strong, silent type—just the way I like 'em."

Jeanie laughed at me. "Rosie, you like *every* type. Strong, silent. Weak, noisy. You just like *boys*—especially good-looking ones."

"I used to like boys. Now I just like one boy. What a drag. I haven't had a date in days. And look at him. He hasn't even noticed I'm here. Maybe this isn't such a good idea, Jeanie. Maybe I ought to resign."

She put her hand on my shoulder. "Don't be silly, Rosie. Harry's just absorbed in his selling warm-ups. He's like this every day. None of us can speak to him until after he's had his first customer. It's like his breakfast. He has to eat someone before he becomes civil."

"But I want him to talk to me. I work here now, after all. I want him to notice *me*."

"Be patient, Rosie."

"I can't. I'm date crazy. I need some attention."

"You're spoiled."

"You're right," I said. "And don't you wish you were too? But I have a great idea! Watch this. If Harry won't talk to anyone until after his first customer, then that means the first person he speaks to is his first customer. And so . . ."

I went out through the back of La Maison de Trash and walked around to the front where Harry was sniffing for customers.

I went right up to him and I asked, "Excuse me, but do you have any Love-oscopes?"

Harry was rubbing his hands together before he even realized who I was. "Of course we have . . ."

Then he saw it was me.

"Oh, Rosie," he said. "I don't think we have enough Love-oscopes for *you*. Not for all the men in your life. But let me check." And he shouted out, "Jeanie, do we have a gross of Love-oscopes back there?" Without waiting for an answer, he said to me, "Even if we do have a gross, that's only twelve dozen—a hundred forty-four—so it probably won't be enough. Just how many did you have in mind?"

"Oh, about one."

"*About* one?"

"Just one, then. An even one."

"An even one," Harry repeated. "Who's the lucky fellow?"

"Someone I love."

"You're in love?"

"I think so."

"You don't know?"

"It's the first time I've ever been in love."

"The first time?" Harry looked as if he'd been struck by lightning. "I thought you went out with anyone who asked you."

"Oh, I do. Or I did. But that doesn't mean I was in love. This is the first time for me. And it's wonderful. And terrible. As I said, I don't know how it's supposed to feel. Do you?"

"Me? No. I'm immune." That was all Harry could say to me. There I was, baring my inner being to him. And all he could say was what he'd said a million times before—he was immune to love. And then, to be sure I wouldn't probe any deeper, he shouted, "Hey, Jeanie, how you coming on that gross of Love-oscopes?"

"No luck," Jeanie shouted back.

"I told you," I said, "I'll take just one. May I have my Love-oscope, please?"

Harry went over to the love section of La Maison de Trash, where there were love cards and love potions and love meters and love charms and love lotions and love rings that changed color as you got closer to or farther away from the object of your desire, and love tests and love litmus paper and love candy that tasted sweet or sour depending on whether you were really in love with the person you thought you were in love with and love lockets and about two hundred things in the shape of a heart, as if your heart really had anything to do with love, and love poems and love statues of Cupid (for the religious) and love gum for mutual chewing and Love-o-grams and love sayings on little cards that you could read to your lover when you couldn't think of anything else to say and, of course, Love-oscopes.

Harry brought me one. I longed for him to put it into my hand, and maybe touch my fingers with his fingers. But he just placed it on the counter.

I wasn't going to let his distant attitude bother me. Not anymore. I had him where I wanted him now. I was going to be by his side every day, day in and day out, or at least when we weren't both in school.

I picked up the Love-oscope. "So what's your birthday?" I asked.

"What difference does it make?"

"Harry, how do you expect me to buy this Love-oscope if I can't test it out?"

"That's ridiculous," he said. "We don't allow people to try the things we sell. What if they try them and then they don't want them? Then we're selling used goods. And La Maison de Trash doesn't sell secondhand. January fourth."

"What?"

"That's my birthday. January fourth. Isn't that what you wanted to know?"

"Yeah. Sure. Okay. Let's see."

I dialed the Love-oscope to match January fourth with May twenty-sixth, which is my birthday.

"What are you doing?" asked Harry.

"Matching birthdays."

"Whose?"

Here was the big test. "Mine and yours."

"Don't do it!" Harry screamed.

I almost dropped the Love-oscope. "Why not?"

"It'll probably break the thing. And then you'll have to pay for it whether you want it or not. See that sign over there: You Break It, You Take It."

"I'll take my chances." I kept dialing until my birthday and his were matched up. Then I looked at what it said.

"Oh, my God!" My face must have registered my shock, too. Harry actually stared into my eyes.

"So what does it say?" he asked.

"None of your business."

He reached for the Love-oscope, but I wouldn't let him have it.

"I'll figure it out for myself," he said. He walked over to the love section and came back with another Love-oscope. "So what's your birthday?" he asked.

"That's none of your business, either." I just couldn't tell him. I knew that if he ever saw what the Love-oscope said about us, it might ruin forever our chance to be together. "But what *is* your business," I went on, "is that I'll take this Love-oscope. How much is it?"

"Four ninety-five, plus tax." Harry held out his hand for the money. All I really felt like doing was taking it and holding it and walking off into the sun that was coming down through the huge skylights over Plainview Mall.

"Is that with the employees' discount?" I asked.

"What are you talking about?"

"I work here now."

"What?"

"I have a job here now."

"Who?"

"Who? Me, Rosie, that's who."

"Here?"

"Here."

"You?"

"Me."

"Mom! Dad! Jeanie!" Harry hollered. "What's this all about? What's going on here?"

Jeanie and Mrs. Higgins came over to us. Mr. Higgins stayed right where he was, taking inventory of some Mexican jumping beans that were very frisky, although they were made in Macau.

"Rosie's working here now," said Jeanie. "Isn't that wonderful?"

"Wonderful?" said Harry. "It's terrible."

I heard him, but I didn't care. He wasn't going to drive me away again the way he did last night.

"Well," said Mrs. Higgins, "we've hired Rosie. So I suggest you accept that fact and get used to her."

"But I can't stand . . ."

He couldn't stand me? I thought I was going to run away. He couldn't stand me?

"I can't stand to be around her."

No, I wasn't going to let him get to me. After all, sometimes I couldn't stand to be around him either. He was too gorgeous sometimes. He made me feel like a bread crust on the plate of life. He made my eyes burn and my hands shake. I couldn't *stand* being near him. But I was just going to have to get used to it.

And he was going to have to get used to me.

"That wasn't a very nice thing to say," Mrs. Higgins told Harry.

"I don't care," he said. "It's true. And besides, how do we even know she knows how to sell. We have a tradition here. This is La Maison de Trash. We are the Higginses. We can sell oil to the Arabs. We can sell salt to the sea. We can sell clouds to the sky. We can sell aerosol to the ozone layer. We can sell milk to a cow. We can sell—"

Mrs. Higgins raised her hand for him to stop. "But *she*"—and now Mrs. Higgins pointed to me—"she can sell invisible ink. *Our* invisible ink. *Invisible* invisible ink. Whole *jars* of invisible ink. *Every* jar of invisible ink."

"She can?"

Mrs. Higgins nodded proudly.

"You can?" Harry said to me.

I nodded pretty proudly myself.

He started to smile at me. Then he caught himself. "Big deal," he said. "What's so hard about selling our invisible ink? It's invisible, after all. Any idiot can see that just by looking into the jar."

"But that's the whole point, Harry," said Jeanie. "The jar is empty. Stop being so difficult."

"Oh, it's all right," I said. "I agree with Harry. It's no big deal. But Harry," I said, right to him. "Harry, here's something for you. It's a brand-new item. How about it, Harry? Want one?"

I held it in my hand. He couldn't see it. But I could see he was dying of curiosity.

"What is it?" he said.

I opened my hand up at the very same time I said, "It's a President Reagan locket!"

Harry stared into my hand. He was transfixed. "A President Reagan locket! Let me see it."

He reached for it. But I closed my hand around it again.

"That'll be two ninety-five," I said. "Plus tax."

"What about the employees' discount?" he asked.

"Of course," I replied.

"Sold!" said Harry.

"Hooray!" screamed Jeanie, and both she and Mrs. Higgins burst into applause.

28

Well, it didn't turn out to be a day when Harry and I fell into one another's arms.

Harry worked his side of the booth. And I worked mine.

The only link between us was the fact that he wore the President Reagan locket I'd sold him. But I didn't think he wore it because of me. He wore it because that way he could get his customers to look at it around his neck as he opened it up—what a great sales technique, not to have it in his hand but around his neck!—and when they looked up toward his neck, they couldn't avoid his incredible eyes, and that was it. Sold! Harry unloaded over twenty President Reagan lockets that day, all to teenage girls. (On the other hand, his sale of love potions suffered when the girls spent their money on the lockets instead.)

He didn't say a word to me all day. If it hadn't been for Jeanie—and for my customers, of course—I would have been as lonely in La Maison de Trash as I was at home.

Jeanie talked to me about Spud. About how after Harry had gotten rid of Stud the night before, she and Spud had danced until almost midnight, with Harry keeping a close eye on them the whole time, of course. And then they all went back to the store, where Mrs. Higgins had been waiting for them with her 3-D camera.

"So was Spud wearing his potato suit when you brought him to meet your mother?"

"Of course he was. Don't you think I would have told you if I'd seen him *without* his potato suit?"

"What did your mother say when she saw him?"

"Nothing."

"Nothing?" I couldn't believe it. How could a girl introduce her mother to her date—the first date in her life! —when that date is dressed like a huge potato, and the mother says nothing?

"Well, not really nothing, Rosie. She said 'hello' and 'nice to meet you' and all that. But she didn't say anything about the way Spud was dressed. At least not then."

"What do you mean, 'not then'?"

"Well, later, of course, at home, she *did* say something."

I grabbed Jeanie's sleeve. "So tell me. Stop holding back. What did she say?"

"She said, 'Idaho or Maine?' "

"She wanted to know what kind of potato he was?"

"Sure. What's so strange about that? I mean, from what I've read in books and magazines and from what you've told me yourself about dates, parents are always asking all sorts of intimate things like is your date Jewish or Catholic or is he Italian or Irish or black or white or yellow. Well, my mother sees I'm going out with a potato, so naturally she asked me if he's an Idaho or a Maine."

"Oh, sure," I said. " 'Naturally.' And what did you say?"

"Nothing. I was laughing too hard."

"How come?"

"Because my mother was laughing too hard. As soon as she said, 'Idaho or Maine?' she burst out laughing. So did my father."

"Your father was there, too?"

"Sure. He met Spud. They both did. They even had their pictures taken with him. We all did. Look. Of course these aren't the 3-Ds—they have to be developed. But we took some Polaroids, too." She reached into her pocketbook and took out some shots of her and Spud, Spud and her parents, Spud and Harry, and one shot of Spud and Harry and her. Spud had his arm around Jeanie. So did Harry.

It made me suddenly sad to look at that picture. "That's how I feel," I said.

"Like a girl trapped between her brother and a potato?"

"No. Like Harry's sister. He hasn't said a word to me all day."

"Me either."

"That's what I mean."

Jeanie looked longingly at a photo of her and Spud before she put all the photographs back in her bag and said, "I see what you mean, Rosie. But that's the way Harry is. You know that. Harry's immune. But if anybody can get to him, it's you. You're the most experienced girl in the world. And you're the most wonderful too."

I gave Jeanie a big hug. "Thank you, Jeanie. I really needed to hear that. I mean, I need you as a friend now more than ever. Not just because of Harry. But because of myself. I mean, I've given up boys. My mother's found a boy of her own, so to speak. And Harry won't even speak to me. So it's you. You and me. You're all I've got."

Jeanie hugged me back. "God, Rosie, what an incredible thing for you to say. And what an awesome responsibility. I don't think I can . . ."

And of course she couldn't. I knew that. "Don't worry, Jeanie. I was just going to ask you what you're doing tonight. I mean, I was going to ask you that as a way of asking you if we could do something together. But you're busy, right?"

Jeanie looked at me with sad compassion. "Right."

"With Spud, right?"

Now her look changed to one of the anticipation of joy. I used to try to look that way before my dates, but I never could manage it. Jeanie didn't have to try. "Right. Of course you could come along with us if you want. Spud would love that, I know. He really likes you—especially after I told him that you didn't run away from us last night because of the way he was dressed."

"You always make me laugh," I said.

"That's what friends are for."

"And love makes me cry."

"Oh, Rosie." Jeanie hugged me again.

"Oh, Jeanie."

At that moment a flashbulb flashed. We both looked up from our hug, and another flashbulb flashed.

It was Mrs. Higgins, taking our picture with her Polaroid camera.

"Your first day here, Rosie. I thought I would capture it for posterity. Smile, Rosie." And this time she took a picture of me alone.

Then Mr. Higgins got into the act. He came over and took the camera from Mrs. Higgins and took a picture of her with me and Jeanie. Then Mrs. Higgins took a picture of Mr. Higgins with me and Jeanie.

Only one person was missing. And how I longed to have my picture taken with him.

But when Mrs. Higgins asked him to come over to have his picture taken, he said, "I'm busy with my customers." And that was that.

It made me all the more sad. I couldn't even bear to look at the pictures.

"Here, take this home to your mother," said Mrs. Higgins, handing me the photograph of me alone. "Let her see the historic picture of you on your first day of work."

"Thanks." I took the photograph and looked at it and saw an unhappy girl named Rosie who had made a terrible mistake. It was bad enough to be in love with somebody who hardly knew you existed (except in those few moments when he did know you existed and he said he couldn't stand to be around you). It was even worse to be in love with somebody who you just got a job working next to and he still didn't know you existed.

I didn't want the photograph, and I didn't want my mother to see it, either. So I slipped it beneath the counter when no one was looking. Let it gather dust like so many other things in La Maison de Trash.

29

Of course I didn't go out with Jeanie and Spud on their date that night. I knew it was more important for Jeanie to have time alone with Spud than for me to be saved from my loneliness and my failure to attract Harry's attention even as we worked together in the same tiny store.

I was planning to work so late that I'd wear out the whole Higgins family except for maybe one member. I figured that if Mr. and Mrs. Higgins went home, and Harry and I were left to close up the place, he'd *have* to pay some attention to me.

But suddenly Harry announced that he was leaving.

It took everyone by surprise.

Mr. Higgins looked at his Grandfather Clock wristwatch. "It isn't even seven-thirty."

Mrs. Higgins said, "You haven't left here before midnight on a Saturday since I don't know when."

And Jeanie said, "Where are you going, Harry?"

"Out to Lake Wooneemonascetasket."

"What in the world for?" asked Mrs. Higgins.

"Don't ask," said Jeanie. "Lake Wooneemonascetasket is famous."

"For what?" asked Mr. Higgins.

"Don't ask," said Mrs. Higgins.

"Well, how am I going to find things out if I don't ask about them?" asked Mr. Higgins.

"It's a place where couples go," I said. I hoped my voice expressed my sarcastic outrage. He *was* in love. And it *wasn't* with *me*.

"The expert," said Harry. "Of course she's right. It's a place where couples go."

"Heck," said Mr. Higgins, "so's New York City. So's Miami Beach, Florida. What's the reason for anyone to run off to Lake Wooneemonascetasket in the middle of the night?"

"To make out, Dad," said Jeanie.

"To make what out?" asked Mr. Higgins. "The stars in the sky? The lights of Plainview? The aurora borealis?"

"I believe Jeanie's referring to hugging and kissing, dear," said Mrs. Higgins.

"Hugging and kissing?" said Mr. Higgins. "Harry? Hey, that's the best news I've heard since we got confirmation of that shipment of Marvelous Marvin Hagler wigs. Congratulations, son. Who's the lucky girl?"

"Yeah, who's the lucky girl?" I wanted to know. How could she be taking away from me a boy I'd been longing for, even if I didn't know it, for over twelve years? I wanted to sell her the love potion that would make her fall in love with Sam Kinison.

"Who said anything about a girl?" And with that, Harry grabbed an infrared flashlight from its display case and left the rest of us looking bewilderedly at one another within the narrow confines of La Maison de Trash.

"If he's going to Lake Wooneemonascetasket, there has to be a girl," said Jeanie, looking sympathetically at me.

"Let's hope there's a girl," said Mr. Higgins.

"Let's hope there isn't," said Mrs. Higgins, because we women had to stick together.

"Or let's hope she drowns," I said. Then I asked if I could have the rest of the night off. With Harry gone, there was nothing to keep me there any longer aside from my job, and what good was work gained when love was lost?

They let me go, and I rushed home, hoping that I could get there before Professor Fuller came to pick up my mother for their date at Trattoria Freddy. I'd changed my mind. I really wanted to go with them. After all, my mother needed me. I was her lucky charm. Where would she be without me? she'd asked. What would she do without me?

She was at Trattoria Freddy without me. And she was having fun without me.

There was no question about it. The house was empty when I got there. My mother was out on a date, and the house was empty. It was the first time I had ever been alone in our house at night.

I missed everybody. My mother. My father. Professor Stanislaus Fuller. Every boy I'd ever gone out with in my life. And the one boy I wanted to go out with and never would.

So I waited for my mother to come home, the way my mother had been waiting for me to come home so many times.

I wondered if she could have been as lonely as I was now.

I wondered if I would ever be as happy as I imagined she was now, out with Stan, eating and talking and laughing and loving one another.

I had so much to talk to her about. I needed her so very much.

But did she need me?

30

It was after midnight when I heard Professor Fuller's car pull up. I'd been lying on my bed staring at the ceiling and seeing images of Harry float by like Peter Gabriel in a rock video, drifting through the universe of my eyes.

Is it any wonder I jumped up when I heard Stan's car?

I went to the window and peered through the blinds. And there they were, my mother and Professor Fuller sitting on the giant front seat of his car. There was enough room on that seat for them *and* me. I could have fit right there between them. Except they hadn't left me any room. They were sitting together like two teenagers. He had his arm around her and she was staring into his eyes.

I think they were talking to one another. But I couldn't really tell—there wasn't enough light from the street lamp. And I certainly couldn't read their lips. Not that I had to. I knew exactly what they were saying.

"I want to kiss you," was what I knew was coming out of Stan's mouth. (Except most of my dates weren't that couth—they just said, "Gimme a kiss," or they sort of lunged for me without warning.)

"I don't think that's a good idea," was my mother's response (all I ever said was, "That's the most ridiculous thing I've ever heard in my entire life"). "I can't kiss you," I knew my mother was saying. "It isn't right. I'm too old to kiss. I have a grown child. And not only that, but I'll bet she's right up there now in her room, looking out at us through the blinds, and if she sees us kissing, she's going to have a fit. Besides, I respect her feelings too much to let you kiss me. She's my daughter, after all."

And that's when they kissed! I couldn't believe my eyes.

How dare she! Here I was, suffering upstairs from love-sickness over the most gorgeous guy in Plainview, who every girl in town has a crush on and wants to buy love potions for, and he's not only immune to them but he's immune to me, the biggest boy-killer in town, and there's my mother sitting in front of our house in a car after midnight kissing a man she met only a few days ago and who she never would have gone out with in the first place if I hadn't gotten on the phone to arrange a date for her and chaperoned her on her date and been her lucky charm and told her to stand on her own two feet. She'd even wanted me to go with her on her date tonight! And she'd thought I'd betrayed her by not going! Well, who was betraying who now?

I couldn't stand it any longer. They were still kissing. They must have known I was looking down at them. They must have known I'd be waiting up for them: I couldn't very well go to sleep while my mother and her date were out cruising around and getting into who knew what kind of trouble. And now this! Kissing like teenagers in front of our very own house. And at a time when I needed my mother more than I'd ever needed her in my whole life.

I ran from my room, tore down the stairs, slammed out

the front door, and practically threw myself onto the window of the car.

"Good heavens!" exclaimed Professor Fuller.

"Rosie!" screamed my mother.

"We were just . . ." explained the good professor.

"We were just . . ." repeated my mother.

". . . saying good night," they said together.

"Well, was it necessary for you to say good night with your lips pressed together?" I asked in my most innocent fashion.

That's when they stopped acting like teenagers. Instead of sitting there sputtering and trying to explain themselves, they both burst out laughing and fell into one another's arms. They didn't feel they had anything to be ashamed of. It was all right to want to sit together in a dark car on a clear night. It was all right to share a kiss. And it was all right to let a teenager in on it.

"Well, get in," said Stan, as he reached over to open the door for me.

"Sure. Come on, Rosie," said my mother, as she stepped out of the car to make room for me.

"But . . ." I said.

"It's all right." My mom motioned for me to get in.

"Come on, girl," said Stan.

And so I slid slowly onto the front seat, right between my mother and her date, right where I felt I belonged. Never mind that I probably shouldn't have been there, that I had interrupted their date (not to mention their kiss).

They both put their arms around me.

"We were sorry you couldn't be with us today and tonight," said Stan.

"That's right," said my mother. "We had a wonderful time."

"But we missed you," said Stan.

"Oh, we did," said my mother. "Stan loves the house. He signed the lease on the spot. And Trattoria Freddy was almost as good as the other night. And Carlo was just . . . well, Carlo was just . . ."

"Wild with jealousy, apparently," said Stan.

"Oh, he was wicked," said my mother. "He wouldn't speak English at all. Only Italian. We got the feeling he was calling us names when he was pretending to tell us the specials. But we had a wonderful time anyway. That's enough about us. What about you, Rosie? How was your own date, darling? How was . . . how did you describe him? The one boy . . . the only boy . . . the . . ."

"The only boy I've ever loved," I said.

That's when my tears started to fall.

31

We sat in the car under the streetlight, Stan and my mother and I.

At first, they just listened to me as I unburdened my heart. I told them all about my getting the job at La Maison de Trash and about how Harry said he couldn't stand to be around me and how he ran off to Lake Wooneemonascetasket with someone else. "I'm in love with somebody who doesn't love me," I said. "It's the worst feeling in the world. It's even worse than not being in love with anybody at all, and I used to think *that* was the worst feeling in the world. Maybe that's why I went out with so many guys. I was looking for love. Looking all the time. Ever since Dad left. I've felt so lonely. So sorry for myself. So I dated all the time. But of course no guy ever came up to the high standards I set in my mind. And then I discovered my feelings for Harry Higgins. Harry had been there all the time, for twelve years! I guess I've always been in love with him. But I didn't know it. And it's so *trite*—my best friend's brother. The thing was, I could never figure him out. I could picture his face when he was little. He was such a beautiful boy. I can remember that even now. I used to try to impress him—jump rope a thousand times in a row, offer to help him with his homework, even though he was two grades ahead of me and I didn't have a clue about his subjects, even then I'd brag about other boys. I guess that's what drove him away—that and the mere fact that he didn't know I was alive other than as the sidekick his sister played with all the time. I thought he would be impressed by my dating prowess. But all it did was make him think I was less worthy, not more. I guess he was right. But the worst part is that I'm still in love with him—the gorgeous boy he was and the handsome hunk he is now. And I can't get through to him. He doesn't seem to see me any more now than he did when we were little. None of the girls can get through to him. They spend all their money on love potions to try to win him over, and he tells them he's immune to love. And then I go so far as to get a job working at La Maison de Trash, and Harry says he can't stand to be around me. What kind of thing is that to say? I mean, if you were Harry, wouldn't you be able to stand to be around me? Am I that terrible? Maybe I *am* a disease. Maybe . . ."

My mother put her arms around me again. I let my head rest on her shoulder. And while she held me, she talked to me.

"There's nothing wrong with you," said my mother. "You're not terrible. You're not a disease. If anybody's sick, it's Harry."

"What?" I wanted to say. "Harry, sick? How dare you talk about Harry that way?" But then I realized how ridiculous it would sound for me to defend the very boy who was saying terrible things about me and breaking my heart.

Besides, Stan came to Harry's rescue. "I don't know if I'd call Harry sick," he said. "Of course, I've never met this young man. But from Rosie's description of him, I'd have to say he sounds like a very scared young man."

Harry, scared? The only thing Harry could be scared of would be two thousand girls stampeding toward La Maison de Trash all at once and force-feeding him love potions in an effort to unlock the passion he just had to have sealed up someplace in his perfect body and his imperfect heart.

"You're right, Stan," said my mother. "In fact, Harry sounds a lot like Rosie to me."

Like me? Harry? Had love turned my mother's brain into a fount of gibberish?

"Yes, he does," Stan agreed with her. "Rosie dates a lot of boys but doesn't go out with any of them more than once. It's a way of protecting yourself, Rosie. And Harry . . . well, Harry doesn't go out with *any* girls—I doubt he even really went out with a girl tonight—and that's certainly a way of protecting himself."

"Yes, from rejection," said my mother.

Rejection? Harry, afraid of rejection? Harry could have any girl he wanted. Even me. Harry is stunning. Everyone knows that.

"Harry doesn't ask Rosie out because Harry's afraid she'll say no," said Stan.

"That's ridiculous," I said.

"Well, why don't you ask *him* out?" said my mother.

"Because I'm afraid *he'll* say no."

"You see, you are alike, you and Harry," said Stan.

"If Harry asks *me* out, I'll say *yes*. But if I ask him out, what guarantee do I have that *he'll* say yes?"

"None," said Stan.

"That's right," agreed my mother. "None. There are no guarantees when it comes to love," she pronounced.

"And since when did you become an expert on love?" I asked.

"Since you taught me everything you know," she said,

running her hand through my hair. "And since Stan made it all a reality."

They looked at each other across me. Their gazes locked just in front of my eyes. So I let mine lock with theirs. I felt secure. I didn't ever want to get out of that car.

But that car wasn't the real world. That car was just the love car, carrying my mother and Stan to paradise no matter where it went. For me, the real world was at Plainview Mall, in La Maison de Trash, where there awaited a boy who did or didn't love me, who was or wasn't like me, who would or wouldn't ask me out, and who would or wouldn't go out with me if I asked him.

Love was still the mystery it had always been. And always would be. Having a discussion in a car under the moonlight after midnight could not solve the mystery of love. But it certainly could make you feel better.

"Thanks," I said to my mom and Stan. I reached for the door handle. "You two stay here. I'm going up to bed. I have a long day tomorrow. A very long day."

"Then come home to have lunch with us," said my mother.

"Yes, do. Please do," begged Stan.

I didn't say I would, and I didn't say I wouldn't. A girl has to keep her options open. I just slid out over my mother. I gave her a kiss and blew one to Stan through the open window of the car.

By the time I got to the front door and stopped to look back at them, they were sitting squeezed together again on Stan's side of the car. My mother's head was on his shoulder.

By the time I was upstairs in my room and looked out at them again through the crack between my blinds, they were kissing again.

Well, it was easy for them. They weren't teenagers. They didn't know how hard love really is when you always have to hide it behind your fear that the person you love doesn't love you.

3 2

When I got to the mall that Sunday, the whole Higgins family was there. I was late.

"I'm sorry," I said. "I overslept. I was up very late last night."

"Me too," said Harry.

"I was up talking to my mother," I said, telling Harry the truth for once.

"And I was out all alone in a rowboat on Lake Wooneemonascetasket, dreaming of love."

Sure he was. I'll bet he was out on Lake Wooneemonascetasket in a rowboat, but he wasn't all alone, and he sure as heck wasn't dreaming of love, not when he had it lying with her head on his knees and probably rowing the boat at the same time, serenading him with a song while she fed him the sandwiches she'd made for their moonlit tryst and poured him the iced tea she'd brewed from tea leaves she'd gone all the way to India to procure.

"So how *was* your date?" I asked him with as caustic a voice as I could muster in the midst of my anger, despair, and jealousy.

"I told you," he said, "I was out all alone—"

"—in a rowboat on Lake Wooneemonascetasket—" continued Jeanie.

"—dreaming of love," I concluded.

Jeanie and I swapped high tens. Harry stood there shaking his head. At least we could unite against him—two girls were better than one (except when it came to dating the same guy: I wanted to drown whoever it was who had gotten my Harry into a rowboat under the moonlight on the lake famed statewide as the liquid love temple of the Wooneemonascetasket Indians).

But Harry was saved from our joint sarcasm by the arrival of a customer, a fat man who came up to the counter, slammed his fist down on it, and said, "I'm looking for a Bulge Eliminator. I heard you have Bulge Eliminators. Gimme a Bulge Eliminator."

"Of course we have Bulge Eliminators," said Harry, as he made his way over to the man, leaving Jeanie and me alone together.

"So who did he go out with last night?" I asked her immediately.

"I have no idea. He doesn't tell me anything. You know that. He's as much a mystery to me as he is to you. Really, he's the most frustrating person in the world. I don't know how you put up with him. I mean, if Spud was as difficult as Harry, I don't know what I'd do."

I put my hand on Jeanie's shoulder and drew her head close to mine, so I could whisper in her ear. "Jeanie, I hate to tell you this, but Spud *is* a mystery. This is a guy whose face you've never seen. Whose body is very possibly shaped like a huge potato. And whose name is not really even Spud. So how can you—"

"Oh, Rosie, I'm so crazy about him. I can't tell you.

Last night he took me out to eat at the most wonderful restaurant. It was a very fancy place with linen napkins and a huge wine list that Spud insisted on looking at even though all we ended up having were Perriers and about six waiters apiece and it must have cost him about—"

"Sounds like Sacre du Printemps," I said.

"It was!" Jeanie shrieked with delight. "How did you know that?"

"Oh, I was taken there during my dating days. It's a nice place. And it *is* very fancy. So I have to assume that Spud . . ."

Jeanie could read my mind. "No. He still wore his potato suit."

"And they let him in?"

"Well, they tried to stop him, but he told them he was a famous restaurant critic from *Pomme de Terre* magazine and he couldn't afford to be recognized as he went from restaurant to restaurant doing his job, so he had to wear a different disguise every night, and tonight he had chosen to grace what he assumed to be their fine establishment as a huge potato."

"And did they actually buy that?"

"Buy it? It was 'Monsieur Spud' this and 'Monsieur Spud' that. They were practically kissing his warts. I swear, Rosie, he's the funniest, most wonderful guy I've ever known. Not that I've known that many. None, in fact. But who could be better than Spud? Really, I don't care *what* he looks like under that suit. Maybe he has a dread disease or something. Maybe his skin is the color of an avocado. Maybe he has hairy hands. Maybe those are really his own warts. It just doesn't matter to me."

"But aren't you at least curious about what he looks like under that potato skin?"

"Of course I am. But I don't care. He's taught me something important. And I'm lucky I learned it right at the beginning of my dating life. Looks don't mean much. In fact, looks don't mean anything. I can't tell you how much I miss Spud at this very moment. If Sunday weren't his day off I'd ask you to cover for me while I sneaked over to Potato Man just to watch him work. That's how much I miss him. And I know he'll be picking me up here after work, so I'll be seeing him in only eight hours. But I'm still crazy missing him. And why do I miss him? Not for his looks. I just miss *him*. Him. Spud. My big potato man."

I shook my head. Lucky Jeanie. Who would ever have suspected it? Not a date in her life, she starts going out with a guy in a potato suit, and she ends up the happiest girl in Plainview. She certainly deserves it. She was the best friend I could ever hope to have. Just the way her strange and distant brother would be the best boyfriend I could ever hope to have.

Why did I want Harry? Why does the flower want the sun? It's far away, though it's always been there; it's beautiful, though it hurts to gaze at it; it warms the heart, though it's painful to touch; it's always been there, though it disappears every night. There wasn't any logic in my wanting Harry, except for the fact that I did. There wasn't any logic in Jeanie's wanting Spud either—at least as far as I could see. But, then, Spud just wasn't my type. He didn't look right, and he certainly didn't dress right. And he himself wanted Jeanie too much for me to be able to want her to be wanted by Spud. There was something wrong with a boy who wanted you more than you wanted him. It wasn't natural. It didn't satisfy a girl's needs to desire what was beyond her—aloof, inaccessible, maybe even immune to her charm and her wiles. They try to teach us in anthro courses and in magazines that *men* are the hunters. I don't buy it. It's girls who must pursue. And yet . . . how nice it would be if Spud were my type. How simple life would be. A nice boy dressed as a potato, probably as funny-looking as his suit. How easy it would be to love the boys who love you. But how could I? Spud—and every Spud in the world—just wasn't my type.

Yet at that very moment, out of the corner of my eye, I saw someone who was. And it wasn't Harry. Thank God it wasn't Harry. Either the first or the second most gorgeous guy I'd ever seen in my life was walking right toward me and Jeanie. Actually I'd place Harry as most gorgeous but this guy was right up there. Maybe he would help me get Harry. Maybe only another gorgeous guy would make Harry jealous.

"Look!" I whispered frantically into her ear as I clutched both her arms in my hands. "There's a guy heading straight in our direction, and he is something to behold."

"Is it Spud?" Jeanie asked excitedly, before I turned her around just in time to come face to face with a tall boy with liquid green eyes and a nose as straight as a knife blade and lips that made you want to investigate them under the microscope of your scientific curiosity and hair like dark thunderheads passing threateningly over your hometown, and, when he spoke, a strangely deep voice like that of a boy who has seen everything and done everything but you are still a surprise to him and you can hear his pleasure in his hot, honeyed voice.

"Hello, girls. I understand you have some love potions for sale around here."

And that's how Eric Levy walked into our lives.

3 3

"Oh, yes," I said. "We have love potions. We have all kinds of love potions. We have love potions for a man to give to a woman to make the woman fall in love with him. We have love potions for a man to give to himself to make him fall in love with a woman. We have love potions for a woman to give to a man to make him fall in love with her. We have love potions for a woman to give to herself to make her fall—"

"That's enough," he said. "I know what I need."

I was disappointed that he'd interrupted me—because I'd memorized every word of the love potion speech that Harry had given to Samantha, the girl from his homeroom whom he'd never noticed. I'd been waiting for an opportunity to recite it, especially if Harry was within earshot. Which he was, though he seemed totally engrossed with the fat man who was looking for a Bulge Eliminator.

On the other hand, if this splendid new guy, on whom I already had a slight crush, knew what he wanted, then who was I to stop myself from selling it to him?

"Fine," I said. "Terrific. Then what'll it be?"

"I'll take the first one you mentioned. That's all. For a man to give to a woman to make her fall in love with him."

"Oh, good," I said. "My favorite. Naturally. I mean, I totally approve of men being aggressive when it comes to women. Don't you?"

"Certainly," he said in that husky voice of his. *Certainly*. There's nothing like a guy who knows what he wants and goes right after it.

" 'Certainly,' " I repeated like any good salesperson, reinforcing the preference of her customer. "And the reason I approve, of course, is that I've been offered this love potion so often myself. Men have given it to me to make me fall in love with them. Right, Jeanie?" I asked her to corroborate, in case this wonderful boy had any reason to be skeptical of my claim.

"Oh, sure," Jeanie said in such a way as to cast a cloud of doubt over the sunshine of my lie. Then she grabbed my head and whispered in my ear, "Fickle, fickle. I thought you loved Harry!"

She smiled at me.

And the guy smiled at her as if to say he and she could both see right through me.

But it wasn't Jeanie who needed anything, I suddenly realized. Here was this fabulous boy buying a love potion directly from me—maybe even for me?—and I wasn't yet turning this at all to my advantage with the man who was the one true love of my life, except he didn't know it yet.

"Could you come over here for a minute, Harry," I called to him.

Harry concluded his sale of the Bulge Eliminator to the fat man—it was a kind of electric blanket that you wrapped around your belly at night and plugged in so the heat would supposedly melt your fat away and after a few mornings you would wake up and be able to see your feet for the first time in years—and came right over to me.

I had him where I wanted him.

"Oh," I said, "I just thought you might help this customer since you're our expert on love potions. And he wants to buy one. A special one. For a special person. But first, let me introduce you. Harry Higgins, this is . . . this is . . ."

I waited for him to say his name. At that moment all I wanted was to hear his lips close over the unique sound of his own identity. I also wanted to know what to call him so I could stop thinking of him only as that gorgeous new boy I'd just met. Who would, I hoped, help me get the most gorgeous boy I'd ever known.

". . . Eric Levy," he said.

Harry looked at Eric Levy. Then he looked at me. Then he looked at Eric Levy again. Then he looked at me.

It was working. Harry couldn't help but think that Eric Levy and I were already compatible, that there was an understanding between us. Maybe we hadn't said much to one another, but surely Harry understood that. Harry never said much either. Handsome boys rarely needed to. They seemed to think their looks spoke for them. And they did. It wasn't fair, but a great-looking face usually removed the need for a fast tongue. That must be why it was the homely boys and the heavy boys who usually had the most to say (except for the understandably shy homely boys, who always seemed to exist in a cocoon of painful silence).

I admitted to myself that Harry had never said a word about wanting me. But if he ever did want me, he knew now that he was going to have to win me away from Eric Levy. Right before his eyes, I was losing my lost heart. (Actually, I was only pretending to lose it, but he didn't know that.) I was out of control, even as I finally felt I was gaining control. I decided that Eric Levy was my magic man, the one love potion that was going to work.

"I think Eric wants a love potion that a man gives to a woman to make her fall in love with him," I explained to Harry. "Isn't that right, Eric?"

"That's right. I need something that works strong and works fast. I don't have any time to waste. I want to be able to give this to a girl, and from that moment on she'll do whatever I want."

"And do you have a particular girl in mind?" I asked him, not in all innocence.

"I certainly do." Thinking of my past I felt there could be little doubt who he had in mind.

Certainly there was no question in Harry's mind. He said to Eric, "May I see some ID please."

"ID?" I couldn't believe it.

"Sure," said Eric, taking out his wallet. He removed his student ID card. I picked it up myself to hand to Harry, except what I really wanted, I admit, was to look at it. I wanted to see Eric's picture. Sometimes you can see a person better in a picture than in reality. You can really get to the bottom of a soul when it's frozen in time and can't juggle features in order to confuse your scrutiny. And Eric certainly looked great in the little photo on his student ID. Even if I'd never met him and had only seen his picture, I could have fallen for him, if I hadn't already fallen for the boy who was now standing there defiantly, obviously trying to keep Eric from buying the love potion that would cast me under his spell forever.

"I think I recognize you," I said to Eric, to cover the fact that I was looking at his photo for so long, and because I actually thought that maybe I did recognize him. "Aren't you an actor?" I figured that whether or not he was an actor, it was the kind of question that would drive Harry crazy.

"Yes, as a matter of fact I am," said Eric.

"Right," I said. "I think I've seen your movies."

"No, I don't think so," he said. "I don't act in movies."

"In what then?" I was genuinely curious all of a sudden.

I mean, there I was, standing next to an actual actor. It was even more thrilling than I'd expected.

"In life," he replied, his voice deeper than ever. He was strange, I had to admit it, but I was beginning to like his mysteriousness and the way he paid attention to me, unlike some people I could name.

Harry couldn't stand him, thank goodness. He scoffed at the statement about being an actor in life and grabbed Eric's ID. "No," said Harry. "This isn't good enough. I need something with your date of birth on it."

"You do?" I was incredulous.

"You can't buy love potions unless you're at least eighteen. State law. Show me something that says you're eighteen."

"I can't," said Eric. "I'm not eighteen. But I don't believe—"

"This is ridiculous," I cut in. Harry had gone too far. I mean, I loved it that Harry had gone too far. It had worked. I'd gotten him jealous over Eric. But at the same time I *wanted* Eric to have the love potion. I wanted him to want me. I wanted everyone to want me . . . maybe that was my fatal weakness.

"Here." I handed him the love potion. It was a beautiful aquamarine color. No woman would be able to resist it. "That'll be two ninety-eight, plus tax," I added, feeling a little silly having to charge him for it, except that, after all, I did work there. I figured I'd reimburse him for it once he gave it to me.

"Thanks," said Eric. "I appreciate it." He gave me a five-dollar bill. As I handed his change to him, I kept my hand out to make it easier for him to slip me the love potion without embarrassing himself by having to force it on me.

"For you," he said.

He handed the vial to Jeanie, who'd been standing there quietly watching the scene.

34

What was going on here? First Spud, now Eric. Was I losing my touch? It was one thing to be passed up by a huge potato. It was another thing to be passed up by someone you could have sworn you'd seen playing the romantic lead in a full-length motion picture.

And look at Harry. All my best-laid plans had gone to waste. He was standing there with a smug smile on his face where a moment before there had been something approaching panic. A guy who was almost as good-looking as him was handing his sister a love potion, and he was actually happy about it. Who knew what it might make her do?

But Jeanie, poor fool, wanted no part of it. "Oh, thank you," she said to Eric. "But I can't. I couldn't. It's very kind of you to offer. And we'll be happy to refund you your full purchase price. But no. I can't take that from you."

"Oh, come on," said Eric. "We both know it's only

symbolic. I mean, I'd give you flowers if I had flowers. But I figured I might need this thing. You're so sweet-looking and kind-looking and obviously nice and quiet and open, I didn't figure I had a chance to win you over if I couldn't get you to take a love potion from me. I know I'm being presumptuous. But I saw you from across the mall, and I just knew I had to get to know you and get you to go out with me. I mean, I don't even know your name, you know. I don't even know . . ."

He let his husky, lovesick voice die out, waiting for Jeanie to pick up his cue.

She didn't. But Harry did. "Jeanie Higgins," he said. "I'm her brother, Harry. Nice to meet you."

Finally, Harry stuck out his hand to Eric. Eric took it. "Yes, we've met," he said.

"Come on, Jeanie," Harry said to his sister. "Talk to this guy. Let him buy you the love potion. What harm can it do?"

"I'm sorry," Jeanie explained to Eric. "But I already have a boyfriend."

"A boyfriend!" Harry put his hand on Eric's shoulder. "She doesn't have a boyfriend. She has a *potato*."

"A potato? What's he talking about?" Eric asked Jeanie.

"It doesn't matter," Jeanie said. "The only thing that matters is that I can't take the love potion from you."

"Forget the love potion," said Eric. "It's only a crutch. A tool. It's just that I lacked the courage to come straight up to you, Jeanie, and to ask you, will you please go out with me tonight. And if you have a date tonight with a potato—or a tomato or a carrot or whatever—then go out with me tomorrow night. Or the night after that. Or the night after *that*."

Jeanie shook her head. "I'm sorry."

"This is ridiculous," Harry said to her. "Say yes to the guy, Jeanie. Go out with him. What harm can it do?"

"Plenty," Jeanie said forcefully to her brother. "I already

have a boyfriend. I'm in love with somebody else. And I won't do anything to jeopardize that relationship. And what I want to know is why are you so anxious to ruin that relationship by forcing me to go out with this boy?"

I thought I knew why. It was because Harry wanted Jeanie to go out with Eric so Eric wouldn't go out with me. Of course, that isn't what Harry said.

"I'll tell you why," he said. "I've gone along with you in all of this so far. You wanted a chaperon, I chaperoned. A guy in studs is picking a fight with your boyfriend, I get rid of the guy in studs. I'll do anything for you, Jeanie. You're my sister and I love you. But the guy you're going out with dresses up as a potato! How do you think that makes me feel? It's bad enough to have to chaperon your own sister. But when her date's a potato! It's hard enough to put up with the fact that your sister is starting to date in the first place, especially when she's younger than you and you haven't even dated yourself. But when your sister's date is a potato, it's twice as hard. It makes me feel like a fool. I'm the guy whose sister is becoming famous all over the mall as the girl who's going out with an ugly potato. And I'm becoming famous as the guy who not only lets his sister date a potato but who even escorts the two of them around. So what's wrong with going out with this guy? He looks normal, doesn't he? He tried to get you to take a love potion, didn't he? I mean, compared to your potato boyfriend, Eric here seems perfect. The two of you seem made—"

"But I'm in love with *Spud!*" Jeanie shouted.

"Spud?" said Eric. "Your boyfriend's name is Spud? And he's a potato? I mean, forgive me for laughing," he said as he pressed his hand across his forehead, "but that guy sounds like a jerk."

"Exactly!" said Harry. "You and I really agree on all of this, Eric. And I swear, the two of you seem what I was just telling my sister—made for each other. Here. Wait here. I'll prove it. Don't move. I'll be right back."

Harry ran off toward the counter where all the La Maison de Trash's love items were stored. He came back with a Love-oscope and shoved it into my hand and said, "You show them how to use it. I've got to make a phone call."

"A phone call?" I couldn't believe it. Who was it to? I was instantly jealous.

"Sure," said Harry. "A phone call." He looked at his watch. "It's eleven-thirty."

"So what?"

"So I have to make a phone call."

"Who to?" I didn't care about showing my jealousy.

"Ellen."

"Who's Ellen?"

"None of your business."

"Why at eleven-thirty?" I had visions of this Ellen waiting by the phone for Harry to call.

"She's waiting by the phone for me to call."

I wanted to strangle him. I wanted to wrap my arms around his neck and squeeze.

3 5

Harry disappeared quickly into the little office where the phone was.

I strained to hear him, but I couldn't. Maybe there was no Ellen. Maybe he didn't really have to make a phone call at all. Maybe he was just trying to escape the fireworks when the Love-oscope showed that Eric and Jeanie weren't made for each other and Eric and I *were*.

"So what's your birthday?" I asked Eric.

"February third," he replied.

"Mine's May twenty-sixth," I said.

Eric ignored me. "What's yours?" he asked Jeanie.

"I'm sorry, Eric. But I'm not playing this game. I told you. I have a boyfriend. I don't need another one. And that's that!"

"I understand that, Jeanie. I really do. And I respect that. But a guy in a potato suit? A guy who calls himself

Spud? You can do better than that. I mean, there has to be something wrong with a guy like that. He's got to be at least a little weird. And who knows what he's like under that suit. What if he's deformed or something? What if that potato suit actually *improves* his looks? What if—"

"Don't you understand, Eric? I don't care what he looks like. Looks don't mean *anything* to me. Nothing."

I thought Jeanie might be carrying things a bit too far with a statement like that. But she and I were different that way. In fact, that's why Eric Levy and I seemed perfect for one another, not that I would give up my pursuit of Harry for Eric, since Harry was the major crush in my life and was my best friend's brother and I'd known him for years and I'd only just begun to stop being afraid of him, maybe, and he was even better looking than Eric, or almost better looking, or maybe it was a dead heat.

So that's when Eric showed he was just like me by saying to Jeanie, "But how can you say looks don't mean anything? How can you say you don't care what this boyfriend of yours looks like? What if there's something *evil* in the way he looks? What if you have children together and the children look like potatoes too, all covered with warts and stringy things and patches of skin like sandpaper? What if—"

Jeanie laughed. "If Spud and I ever have children, they will be beautiful no matter what they look like. But we met only a couple of days ago. So it's kind of early to talk about children. And as for—"

"But if I were Spud, I'd want to have children with you," Eric said. "I think you're the most beautiful girl I've ever seen. And the most wonderful. All I had to do was look at you once, from across the mall, and I thought I'd probably want to spend the whole rest of my life with you."

I didn't know how she could do it, but Jeanie ignored the incredibly beautiful things Eric was saying and went right on with her previous thought, just as I was about to try to convince her that the least she owed herself was to check out how she and Eric performed together on the Love-oscope. "And as for Spud's being evil," she continued, "*you're* the one who's evil, Eric Levy. You're not evil for coming over here and trying to get me to go out with you. But you are evil for trying to get me to go out with you after I tell you that I have a boyfriend and he's the only one I'm going out with *period*. And that's it. Understand?"

"I understand," said Eric. "But I don't accept it. Because I think you're the evil one, Jeanie. You're the evil one for not even giving me a *chance*. That's all I ask. That's all anyone can ask. And that's what everyone *should* ask. A chance. One single, solitary chance. It's one thing to be shot down after you've had a chance to fly. But to be shot down before you've even left the ground—it's cruel. It's terrible. It's inhuman. It's *evil*. One chance. That's all I ask. One date. Come on, Jeanie. What do you say? Please. I beg of you. One date. And then, if you never want to see me again, I'll disappear forever from your life, and no one will be the wiser. Except for me, of course. I'll be older and wiser, knowing I fell in love with a girl who was just too good for me. Come on, Jeanie. One date. That's all I'm asking. Once. One date. Please."

His persistence was beautiful. If some boy had ever spoken to me like that, I probably would have gone out with him not once but twice. I didn't see how Jeanie could resist him now. He'd put his life in her hands. She was the complete mistress of his destiny.

But Jeanie just shook her head. "I'm sorry," she said. "I'm sorry."

At just that moment, Harry rushed back from his supposed phone call. He grabbed the Love-oscope out of my hand and said, "So what did this say?"

"Nothing," said Eric. "Your sister wouldn't tell me her birthday. Do you know her birthday?"

"Sure I do. I'll do it." Harry hurriedly turned the dials on the Love-oscope. "Oh, my God!"

It was exactly what I'd said when I'd looked at the match of Harry's birthday and my own on the Love-oscope.

"What does it say?" Eric asked desperately.

But just like me, Harry wouldn't say. I could only guess at the message. But if it said about Eric and Jeanie what it had said about Harry and me, then it was no wonder Harry wanted to keep it secret.

He put the Love-oscope very gently into his pocket. "Sorry," he said to Eric. "I can't show it to you. But look, how about one of these?" And he pointed to the President Reagan locket around his neck.

"What's in it?" asked Eric.

"President Reagan," said Harry.

"What, are you kidding?" Eric was astounded.

"Here, take a look at mine," said Harry. "It's customized. For a little extra, maybe I can get you a customized one too."

"What is it? President and *Mrs.* Reagan?"

"Take a look," said Harry, "just take a look." He shielded the locket with his hands so only Eric could see it when he opened it.

Eric looked. Then he looked over at me and then over at Jeanie. "Hey," he said to Harry, "can you get me a customized one, too?"

"Sure," said Harry. "Of course, it'll cost you extra."

"Whatever it costs, I'll pay," said Eric. He took out his wallet.

"Come back this afternoon," said Harry. "I'll have it ready for you then."

That Harry, he was the greatest salesman in the world. He could sell anything, even a specially-customized President Reagan locket to a guy who hadn't wanted a President Reagan locket in the first place.

I felt like throwing myself into Harry's arms. Not only would that demonstrate what kind of a super salesman I thought he was, but it would also show Eric what he was missing when he chose Jeanie over me.

But I didn't.

I wasn't going to throw myself at Harry until I knew he was ready to catch me.

36

Jeanie asked me to take a walk with her. She didn't just ask. She begged.

"Please," she said. "I've got to get out of here. I've got to talk to you, Rosie."

I couldn't figure out Jeanie's panic. Everything was back to normal:

Mr. and Mrs. Higgins were both working the counters.

Harry was selling our newest item—musical hair barrettes—to a steady stream of girls.

And Eric was gone, not to return until later, when Harry was going to have his customized President Reagan locket ready for him.

"Sure," I said to Jeanie. "I'll take a walk with you—if it's all right with your parents. But why? What's the matter?"

"I'll tell you. I'll tell you." Jeanie pressed her hand on my arm. Her fingers dug into my skin. It hurt. I didn't know if she was hanging on in this desperate way because she needed me or if she suddenly hated me for trying to grab Eric Levy for myself before she had a chance at him, not that she actually wanted him—poor, foolish, faithful Jeanie.

She signaled to her parents that we were going to take a break.

"We don't have much time," said Jeanie. "Come on." Her fingers still in my arm, she pulled me out into the mall. But it wasn't the way it used to be between us when we strolled arm-in-arm like two carefree ladies with nothing more on our minds than the possibilities of love.

It was still love, of course, that occupied us. But now we were desperate, not carefree. Now we knew more and therefore suffered more. Now we were in pain from the very thing that brought us our greatest pleasure: boys, boys, boys, boys, boys.

"Shall we go to The Scarlet Pumpernickel?" I asked, naming the most sophisticated sandwich store in the mall.

"I'm not hungry," Jeanie answered. "The only place I really feel like going to is Each Sold Separately."

That's when I knew something was really wrong with Jeanie. We only went to the toy store when we wanted to pretend to be little girls again and could tell each other our deepest, darkest secrets that were so bad and so disgusting that only by recapturing the innocence of childhood, which thank goodness we had left far behind, could we forgive one another.

So as we walked through the endless corridors of toys and games and huge stacks of the latest in disposable baby wetness-protection devices, Jeanie confessed:

"I like Eric Levy."

"Thank goodness," I replied. "For a while there I was worried about you, Jeanie."

"But I feel so bad. I feel so guilty." She put her hand on my arm to stop me. She turned me toward her and looked deeply into my eyes. Behind her I could see a stack of plastic teddy bears called Classic Cubs. I felt like a teddy at that moment, ready to give comfort.

"Oh, don't feel bad," I said. "Don't feel guilty. I didn't want Eric that much anyway. I was just using him to try to get Harry jealous. And it was obviously you he was—"

"I don't feel guilty about taking him away from you, you silly girl. I feel guilty about Spud."

"Spud?" I couldn't believe my ears. "What does Spud have to do with this? It's Spud's day off. He's not even around. And wherever he is, he's probably sitting there in his potato suit wondering how he got a beautiful girl like you to fall in love with him in the first place and thanking his lucky stars and biting whatever kind of fingernails potatoes have worrying about what's going to happen when he finally has to reveal himself to you."

"But he already has revealed himself," Jeanie said. She started walking down the aisle, past all the other plastic animals, including a monkey family caught in a huge embrace. "He's kind and gentle and fun and loyal. Which is more than I can say for myself. I don't know what it is about me. I think I have a boyfriend, and I'm never, ever going to want another boyfriend. And along comes someone like Eric Levy and what happens to me? I'm attracted to him, I like him. I want to go out with him."

"That's not the way it sounded to me, Jeanie. That guy was begging for you to go out with him, and all you did was say no."

"I said no. But I didn't mean no."

"Golly, you really are different from me, Jeanie. My whole life, I said yes, but I didn't mean yes."

Even in her confusion and despair, Jeanie laughed at me. "I *am* different. And I'm the same. All girls are different. And all girls are the same. I'm just so *mixed up*, Rosie."

"Me too," I confessed.

"Let's go over here." Jeanie took my arm.

We walked together over to what Each Sold Separately advertised as The World's Largest Wall of Dolls. On one whole wall of the store, which was about a hundred yards long, hung dolls of every size and color and outfit and expression and cuteness and capability. It was like seeing all of humanity before you and you could take your pick and have anyone you wanted. Too bad life wasn't like that—but I guess that was why dolls were invented.

Jeanie and I were thinking the same thought.

"Life used to be so easy," she said.

"When we were young."

"Before boys."

"Before *certain* boys."

"Before Spud. Before Eric."

"Before Harry."

"So now what do we do?" she asked.

"Well, we could each buy one of these dolls. And take them home. And live with them for the rest of our lives. And remain little girls. Or—"

"Or we could go back and deal with our boyfriends."

"Exactly my sentiments," I agreed.

"But . . ." she said.

"But . . ." I said.

What boyfriends? Which boyfriends? Whose boyfriends?

"Let's be practical about this," I said. "Eric is coming back this afternoon to get the customized locket that Harry's making for him. And that's the perfect time for you to tell him that you want to go out with him after all."

"But what about—"

I could read her mind. "Don't worry about Spud. It's Spud's night off. Spud isn't here. Spud doesn't even exist. I mean, he doesn't exist if he isn't wearing his potato outfit. And if he *is* wearing it on his day off, then you're in a lot more trouble than I already think."

Jeanie still wasn't convinced. I guess she just didn't

realize how great Eric Levy really was. "But I love *Spud*," she said.

"And I love Harry," I said. "But where is that getting me? Believe me, Jeanie, if Eric Levy asked me out the way he asked you out, I'd say, 'Where, when, and how often?' "

"But Harry isn't Spud."

No kidding, Jeanie. I didn't know whether to be grateful or miserable that Harry wasn't Spud. Of course Spud wasn't exactly my type. But Spud loved Jeanie. And who knew how Harry felt about me? To him, I was just another disease doing battle with his immune system, and there was no health insurance against the mad passion of a thwarted girl.

"I wonder what the Love-oscope said about you and Eric," I said. "Don't you?"

"Not particularly. I don't believe in those things, Rosie. They're just like horoscopes. They're just another form of superstition. I can't tell you how many silly boys and girls I've seen buy those things and match their birthdays and if the Love-oscope tells them they're made for each other, they stand there kissing, and if the Love-oscope tells them the only thing they have in common is sweaty palms, they think they've made a terrible mistake and they walk away like strangers. That's no way to decide who you love and who loves you."

"But Jeanie, I *know* what the Love-oscope said about you and Eric."

She grabbed my arm. Then she looked down at her hand. She didn't want it to be her hand. She didn't want to be just another silly girl. "You do?"

I nodded.

"Don't torture me, Rosie. Tell me. Even though I don't want to know. Even though I don't believe in it for a minute. Tell me. Tell me."

I had to tell her. She was the best friend I had in the world. "Well, to judge from Harry's reaction, the Love-oscope said the same thing about you and Eric that it said about me and Harry."

"What's that?" Her fingers were still on my arm. In another moment, they would be *in* my arm.

"The Love-oscope said, 'You Will Get Married and Have Many Beautiful Children.' "

"Oh, my God!" said Jeanie.

37

I went home that fateful Sunday to have lunch with Mom and Stan.

They were closer than ever. Now they didn't sit outside in a car and steal kisses in the darkness.

Not that they kissed in front of me. Not that they even held hands. But I knew they were kissing in their minds. They were holding hands in their minds. I didn't have to read their minds to know this. I could just tell. It was in their looks. It was in their voices. It was in their smiles at one another. It was in the way they were with one another when they were in the same room.

Things were so *easy* between them. They'd only just met, and here they were kissing in broad daylight in their minds. I'd known Harry for years, and we were no closer to kissing now than we'd been since childhood.

It was so much easier to be an adult than a teenager, I thought. Love came so much quicker and smoother.

But then I realized that Stan would be going back to New York City right after Christmas, when the family came back to their house and his lease ran out.

Poor Mom, I thought.

What a louse Stan was, I thought.

How could he just leave her?

How was I going to be able to take care of her then?

She was going to need me again, the way she needed me to get her a date with Stan in the first place.

Mom was in full control of herself now. She was once again the mother in the family. But come Christmas, she would be a young girl again, and I was going to have to take over the family and run her love life.

Poor Mom. Maybe it was easier to be a teenager after all. Except Harry and I hadn't gotten to kiss or hold hands even in our minds. Or only in my mind. And there was nothing more lonely or forlorn than a mind that was in love all by itself.

My mom had made a wonderful lunch. It was very fancy—paper-thin smoked salmon with a dill-mustard sauce, skinny little cold string beans vinaigrette, warm sourdough baguettes with saga blue cheese, all served with a bottle of Chardonnay from Australia.

It was nice to have a man in the house again.

And yet I was still filled with a feeling of sadness and loss. Not just over Harry. Over Stan, too. We were both going to lose him, my mother and I. He would be going away no matter what we did to please him.

Men. They were all the same. Either they didn't love you in the first place, like Harry, or they took their love away and went back to the big city, like Stan.

But in the midst of this glorious meal and this happily sad occasion, my mother said something that made me forget about how bleak our future looked.

"Oh, Rosie, I forgot to tell you. I had the strangest phone call this morning."

"That's right," said Stan. "A boy called you."

"A boy?" My heart pounded. I couldn't help it. I still got excited at that kind of news, even if I'd given up all boys except for one.

"I hope it wasn't Jack Trumbull."

"It wasn't," said my mother.

"Or Steve Pease."

"No."

"Good. Or Bruce Ashworth. Or Paul Ashworth if he decided to change his name back to Paul."

"Someone changed his name from Paul to Bruce?" said Stan.

"That's right," I said.

"It must be because of The Boss."

"Stan!" I couldn't believe my ears. Professor Stanislaus Fuller knew about Bruce Springsteen?

"It wasn't Bruce *or* Paul Ashworth," my mother said.

"Then who was it?" I couldn't bear the suspense, not that I wanted it to be anybody but the one boy I loved.

"He said his name was Eric. Who's—"

"Eric!" I screamed.

"Apparently he's someone important," said Stan, who had his hands over his ears. He obviously hadn't spent much time with a screeching teenager.

"Who's Eric?" asked my mother.

"Eric's a . . . boy."

"Yes," said my mother. "I could gather that much myself. Even your naive, inexperienced mother could tell Eric was a boy. But *which* boy? I've never heard of Eric before."

"Oh, he's just someone I met today. He's gorgeous, actually. And he's charming and he's got a very deep voice that's so sexy you can't imagine and he's so confident and persistent, you wouldn't believe it. Except . . ."

"Except what?" asked Stan.

"Except it wasn't me he wanted. I mean, I thought it was, just the way I did with Spud, but—"

"Spud?" said my mom. "Spud? Who's Spud?"

"Spud?" Stan was shaking his head. At least he didn't try to pretend Spud was another rock star. "Spud," he said again. "He sounds like a potato."

"He is a potato."

"And you thought he *wanted* you?" Now my mother couldn't believe her ears. I guess it was true what people said—how the generations couldn't really understand one another.

"Yes," I said, "but it *wasn't* me he wanted. It was Jeanie. And now Jeanie and Spud are going out together. Except when Jeanie met Eric, she fell for him. And Eric fell for her too. So you see *that's* why I said it wasn't me Eric wanted. Just the way it wasn't me Spud wanted. It was Jeanie. Both of them wanted Jeanie. And when Harry did their Love-oscope, it said they would get married and—"

"There's that Love-oscope again," my mother said. "That's what *he* was calling about."

"Who?"

"Eric."

"Eric was calling about a Love-oscope?"

Stan held up his hands. "What's a Love-oscope?"

"Eric was calling about a Love-oscope?" I asked my mother again. I was thinking hard, and what I was thinking was making my heart beat out of control.

"Well, not exactly. He didn't tell me about the Love-oscope until I told him I wouldn't tell him what he wanted to know until he told me why he wanted to know it."

"So what was it he wanted to know?" I asked.

"Your birthday," said my mother.

"He wanted to know my birthday?"

"That's right. And I told him I couldn't give out that sort of information until I knew—"

"Yes," Stan said. "And that's when he told you he needed the information for the Love-oscope, Ellen. But *what's* a Love-oscope?"

Ellen! I was too excited to answer. "What time did he call?" I asked. My voice was trembling. So was the rest of me.

"Oh, I don't know," said my mother. "About eleven. Eleven-thirty."

That's when I realized my dreams had been answered. Unless I'd been dreaming all of this. Or dreaming what it meant.

"And did you tell him my birthday?"

"Oh, I hope I didn't do something wrong." My mother looked at me over her wine glass.

"Did you?"

"May twenty-sixth," she said.

"Oh, Mom, you're wonderful." I got up and kissed her. Then I kissed Stan. And then I headed out the door.

"Where are you going?" she asked.

"Back to the mall. Thanks for the delicious lunch."

"But you didn't finish your—"

"You two can kiss each other now. I mean not just in your minds."

"We can what?" said Stan.

"Say hello to Eric for me," said my mother.

"But I thought she was in love with someone named Harry," I could hear Stan say. He was thoroughly perplexed.

"Don't worry, dear. Rosie knows what she's doing."

"So what's a Love-oscope?" he asked.

"I don't have a clue," my mother answered. Then she laughed.

So did he.

I ran out the door to the sound of their happiness.

And toward my own.

38

Everybody was busy when I rushed into La Maison de Trash.

Mr. Higgins was doing a physical count of the mustache-and-sideburn wig sets that so many boys liked to buy right around the time they turned thirteen. And he was grumbling about how the wig company always sent him too many red-hair sets and not enough blond ones.

Mrs. Higgins was demonstrating Snore Stoppers to a large group of men and women who were gathered around her. A Snore Stopper was a kind of rubber cone that fit over a person's nose and was light-sensitive so that it reacted to darkness by tightening up and was guaranteed to stop snoring.

Jeanie was wrapping up the sale of some SAT Nocturnal Preparation Cassettes, which guaranteed higher scores for the Math and English tests if you played them all night on the optional auto-reverse tape machine while you slept.

And Harry was surrounded by girls, as usual, as he sold them Pulse-O-Meters that attached to the love-sensitive pulse-points on their bodies and clicked wildly whenever they were near boys who had crushes on them even if they didn't know those boys or, if they did know them but never cared about them before, they learned the boys cared about them. These were a vast improvement on the old Pulse-O-Meters, that only told you if *you* had a crush on someone else, as if anyone needed a Pulse-O-Meter to tell them that.

Needless to say, each girl bought one and tried it out immediately, in the hope it would tell her Harry had a crush on *her*.

"Don't try it on me," Harry was saying. "I'm immune. But it works on the rest of the world. It's the ideal love detector. You won't ever have to fall in love with anyone who's not in love with you. It's guaranteed. No more heartache. No more uncertainty."

And the girls kept buying.

Harry was incredible. Everybody wanted him, including me. But he wanted nobody.

Except for me.

I knew it now, and I could prove it.

But before I had a chance to apply my new theory of the love of Harry Higgins for Rosie Dupuy, Jeanie saw me and rushed over and said, "Oh, Rosie, I'm so glad you came back. I don't know what I'm going to do."

"About what?"

"When Eric comes back. He's due any moment. For his custom-made President Reagan locket. The one Harry promised him. He's going to come back here to pick it up, and I don't know what I'm going to do."

"Just let Harry sell it to him and—"

"But I can't get him out of my mind. I still like him. It's terrible. I mean, I'm in love with Spud, but . . ."

"Would it make you feel any better to know that when I got home for lunch, my mother told me Eric had called?"

I thought that would cure her. I thought that would get her so angry at Eric that she'd never want to see him again or even hear his name. But I hadn't counted on how love can cloud your vision.

"Oh," Jeanie said, "did he want to ask you about me?"

"It wasn't about you he was calling. It was about me." I didn't want to hurt Jeanie. I just wanted to cure her. That's what she seemed to want. Jeanie was the kind of girl who could love only one boy at a time, even when she loved two. Jeanie was the kind of girl who turned good luck into tragedy. Anyway, my little plan to cure Jeanie through jealousy didn't work. She didn't believe me.

"Oh," she said, "I wish that were true. You're only saying that to make me feel better. I know you, Rosie. You think I'll get over Eric if I think it's you he wants. But it isn't. I know that. A girl can tell these things. He wants me. And I think I want him. And I *know* I want Spud. And I don't know what to do. It's a tragedy. A real tragedy."

I put my arm around my best and only friend. "I know you so well. Only you would think it's a tragedy. So two guys are in love with you. A lot worse things can happen to a girl. Like no one at all being in love with her."

"It's not who's in love with me," Jeanie responded. "I don't even know who's in love with me. It's how *I* feel. I like two boys. I'm all divided inside. I feel terrible. I thought my life was so easy. Me and Spud. And then along comes this guy Eric, and I fight him off and I fight him inside myself, and still . . ."

I didn't know what to say to her. Jeanie was so new at this. I knew every guy in Plainview and had dated practically all of them. But I didn't know what to say to my friend. She had a problem that wouldn't even have seemed like a problem to me, but to her it was very painful, and so it began to be very painful to me.

"Well," I said, trying to cheer her up, "it wasn't Eric who called me anyway."

"But I thought you said it was."

"*He* said it was. He told my mother his name was Eric. But it wasn't."

"It wasn't Spud, was it?" Jeanie seemed in a panic.

I tightened my grip on her shoulder. "Of course it wasn't Spud. Spud never even liked me from the beginning. As you very well know. Besides, how could it be Spud? Spud doesn't even know Eric."

"I know he doesn't. But I *think* he does. Spud knows everything about me. Spud can read my mind. So I think he knows about Eric and how I feel about him."

"But he doesn't. It's only your guilty conscience speaking."

"Oh, Rosie, I know. And that's exactly what I feel. Guilty. It's the most terrible feeling in the world. Guilt. You're so smart. You put your finger right on it. *You're* the one who knows everything." She finally gave me a smile, even if it was just a little one.

"Yeah, sure," I said. "Me, who never felt guilty about anything when it came to boys. Of course, I never cared enough about any boy to feel guilty about going out with any other boy."

"But what about Harry?" Jeanie spoke protectively of her brother, as if he hadn't done everything he could to break my heart. "And what about this other guy who called and said he was Eric. Who was it? Who's calling you now? Was it Bruce Ashworth or Steve Pease or Jeff Keisling or—"

I laughed. "That's just what I asked my mother."

"And what did she say?"

"She said it was Eric."

"And what did she say he wanted?"

"He wanted to know my birthday."

"Your birthday? Why would someone call your mother asking to know your birthday? Is he planning to buy you a car or your birthstone? Hey, we've got every birthstone there is here at La Maison de Trash. Or maybe it's some college admissions dean who knows how smart you are and wants to give you early acceptance. Or—"

"No, it's not anything like that."

"Then what is it, Rosie? Who is it?"

"Well, there's only one person who can answer that mystery."

"Eric," Jeanie pronounced. "It has to be Eric. He had someone call you up using *his* name, and—"

"It's Harry," I told her.

Jeanie couldn't believe it. "Do you mean to tell me that Harry had somebody call you up and pretend to be Eric so . . . I get it. Harry likes Eric, right? And Harry doesn't really think Spud is right for me—because he *is* a human potato and he *does* dress a little strangely. So Harry had somebody call you up so you'd get all excited about Eric and you'd go after Eric yourself, and I'd get jealous and I'd go after Eric once I saw you going after Eric, and then you and I would battle it out over Eric, and in the heat of our battle I'd forget all about Spud so Harry wouldn't have to worry that I'm going to end up with Spud and Harry will have to keep defending my honor because I was dating a potato. I swear it, Rosie, boys are so devious, and my brother is the worst. What an insidious plan!"

"It isn't like that at all, Jeanie. Harry knows who called, but it wasn't to get you jealous."

"So what was it for? Why did whoever it was say it was Eric?"

"Let's ask Harry." I took her arm and we started to walk over to Harry.

He was still surrounded by all the girls, who had their hands up in the air as if they were bidding for Pulse-O-Meters instead of just buying them.

And just as we were getting close to him, Jeanie gasped and grabbed my hand and pointed down the long corridor of Plainview Mall.

"Oh, my God, Rosie! Look! Look who's coming. It's Spud. It's my Spud."

39

And sure enough, there was Spud—huge, awkward Spud, carrying what I knew was a sour cream and applesauce–stuffed potato skin in one mitten and a bunch of flowers in the other.

"I thought it was his day off," I whispered to Jeanie.

"It *is* his day off," she whispered back. "But I don't care. I'm happy to see him. Look at him. He has *flowers* for me, Rosie, flowers. He's the best guy in the whole world."

"But what about Eric, Jeanie? Eric is supposed to show up here any minute too. For his customized President Reagan locket. What are you going to do?"

She looked at me with panic in her eyes. But before she could answer, if there really was any answer she could give, Spud sort of leaped over the counter, banging his huge behind on it, came right over to me and Jeanie, and handed her the stuffed potato skin and the flowers and said to her, "Hello, light of my life."

None of the girls around Harry could believe their eyes. They were laughing and pointing at the gallant Spud. "Who's that?" some of them asked. "What's that?" said others.

"That's my future brother-in-law," Harry said. "Why don't you all try your new Pulse-O-Meters out on *him*?"

And with that, Harry walked away, leaving them, as he tried to leave all of us, forlorn. And leaving their Pulse-O-Meters as quiet as the heart of a lonely girl.

To my surprise, Harry walked right over to us. He usually tried to avoid me. Maybe he'd finally decided to tell his secret.

But no. It wasn't me he wanted to talk to. It was Spud.

"Can I have a word with you?" Harry tried to take Spud aside.

But Spud wouldn't budge. "Whatever you have to say to me you can say to Jeanie."

"Okay," said Harry. "I just didn't want to embarrass you."

"Embarrass me?" Spud was incredulous. "Look at me, Harry. Do I look like someone who can be easily embarrassed?"

Harry tried to give Spud a serious once-over, but he couldn't do it without smiling. "No, I have to admit it. I can't think of anything that would embarrass you. Except a look in the mirror."

"There, you see," said Spud. "So go ahead. Say it. What's on your mind?"

"Well," said Harry, "at any time now, there's going to be a guy coming around here and he's going to be coming to pick this up." Harry reached into his pocket and pulled out a President Reagan locket.

"What's that?" asked Spud.

"It's a President Reagan locket." Harry dangled it in front of Spud's eyes.

Spud laughed so hard I thought his warts would pop off.

And when he was done laughing, he said, "You gotta be kidding, Harry."

"It's a *customized* President Reagan locket," said Harry.

"What's in it, a horse?" Spud went right on laughing.

"Hey," said Harry, "aren't you even interested in who it's for?"

"Who it's for? Harry, you can sell a customized President Reagan locket to anyone who's stupid enough to buy one. And look at you, Harry. Isn't that a President Reagan locket around *your* neck? I mean, if you can wear one . . ."

"Well, it's not just for anybody," said Harry. "It's for—"

Jeanie was clutching my arm. I could tell she felt powerless to stop her brother from telling Spud all about Eric. Or maybe she wanted him to tell Spud all about Eric, to get rid of her guilty conscience.

But I couldn't let it happen, not to my best friend. So I went up to Harry and I took his arms in my hands and I said, "Harry, why did you call my mother this morning?"

"What?" Harry tried to break free from my grip. But I wouldn't let him go. (And I had to admit, his sinewy, strong arms inside his sumptuous sweatshirt felt fabulous in my hands.)

"Why did you call my mother this morning and ask her for my birthday?"

"Your birthday? Why would I want to know—"

"The Love-oscope," I said.

I thought I had him. But Harry came right back at me. "The Love-oscope. That's the most ridiculous thing I've ever heard. The Love-oscope. As if I believed in those stupid things. The Love-oscope. That's just for silly girls and lovesick potatoes like Spud here. I don't need—"

"Harry, I *saw* you. This morning. But I only put two and two together when my mother told me a boy called asking what my birthday is. And then I remembered how you rushed back and grabbed the Love-oscope out of my hand and dialed it and you looked at what it said and you said,

'Oh, my God!' which was the same thing I said when I put our birthdays together and saw what the Love-oscope said."

"So what did it say?" asked Spud.

"It said," I started to say, " 'You will get m—' "

"But that wasn't me who called you. That was Eric. Eric Levy. That's who called you. Eric."

"Aha!" I had him now. "And how would *you* know it was Eric Levy unless it was you *pretending* to be Eric Levy?"

"Who's Eric Levy?" asked Spud.

"Oh, no," cried Jeanie, as if it pained her to her very core to hear the name of her new crush on the lips of her old crush.

"I'll tell you who Eric Levy is." Harry was happy to have the subject changed and he wanted it to stay changed.

"Harry, *don't*," Jeanie pleaded.

"Who's Eric Levy?" Spud asked Jeanie, as if he realized all of a sudden that it was Jeanie he should be asking.

"Eric Levy is the—" Harry began.

Jeanie held up her hand. "No, Harry. I'll tell him. Not you. It's my place to tell him."

Jeanie turned to Spud. She took both his mittens in her hands and looked up into his little eyes.

"Eric Levy is a boy I met today. He saw me and he came over to the shop and he asked me out."

"So did you say you'd go?" asked Spud.

"Of course I didn't, Spud."

"I knew it!" he said triumphantly.

"But I wanted to go." Jeanie was gripping Stud's mittens so hard that his potato skin got all bunched up in her fists. It must have been very hard for her to confess to Spud. I know I could never have done it. I mean, I wanted to go out with Eric Levy myself, but I wasn't standing there saying that to Harry, and Harry and I hadn't even been out on a date in our lives.

Spud couldn't believe his ears. "You what?"

"I wanted to go."

"But why?" Oh, how sad it was to think of the road of misery onto which Spud had just taken his first steps.

"I don't know why. I love *you*, Spud. But there's something about Eric Levy. . . . I just liked him. I thought you were the only boy I could ever like, but I liked him, too."

"Why? Is he better looking than I am?"

"That wouldn't be very hard," said Harry.

Spud gave Harry as dirty a look as a potato is able to give, which is pretty dirty, actually.

"He's gorgeous," Jeanie said simply.

"Is that all you care about?" asked Spud. "Looks?"

"If that's all she cared about, she wouldn't be going out with you," Harry said.

Now Spud looked at Harry as if he'd like to sit on him and bury him in the earth from whence Spud himself had sprung.

"Is that what you think?" Jeanie asked Spud. "That all I care about is looks?"

Now Spud looked down at himself. "I guess not. But if it isn't his looks, what is it?"

"I don't *know*. He was just . . . nice, fun. And he seemed to like me a lot."

"But I like you a lot," said Spud. "And I'm nice, aren't I? I'm fun."

"Yes, you are, you *are*. But so is *he*. Oh, Spud, I don't know what I'm going to do."

"Well." Spud seemed to be gaining his courage. "Are you going to go out with him?"

Jeanie took her hands out of Spud's and stood there looking up at him. I knew her well enough to know what she was thinking. I knew that she knew this was the most important answer to any question she'd ever given in her life.

"No," she said. "No. I'm not going to go out with him."

"You're not?" said Spud, gratefully.

"You're not?" said Harry, disbelievingly.

"You're not?" I said, confusedly.

"No, I'm not," said Jeanie. "I never thought I would. Not while I love you, Spud. But I just wanted to tell you about it. About him. I just had to. I wanted you to know. I wanted you to know me, even if it meant you wouldn't want to see me any longer because I had betrayed you."

"But you haven't betrayed me. You couldn't betray me, Jeanie. You don't even know who I am."

Harry couldn't take any more. He walked over to Spud. "She knows you're a guy who goes around dressed like a potato and won't show his face. For all she knows, you *are* a potato. And my sister is not going to be seen for the rest of her life with a potato next to her."

"Is that so?" said Spud. "Well, I admit, I do have my secrets. But we all do, don't we, Harry. Even you."

"What do you mean, even me?"

"Even you, Harry. For example, that locket you're wearing. That President Reagan locket. Why don't you open it up and show us what's in it."

Harry's hand went up to his neck. He wrapped his fist around the locket. "No, I can't. There's nothing in it."

"Come on, Harry," said Spud. "Show us."

"No."

"Show us the picture, Harry. Show us the picture of the girl, Harry."

Harry couldn't believe it. Neither could I. Girl? What girl?

It was as if Harry could read my mind. "Girl? What girl?"

"Show us the picture of Rosie," said Spud.

Rosie? Rosie. *I* was Rosie. But how could Spud know there was a picture of Rosie in Harry's locket?

"How could you know there's a picture of Rosie in my locket?" Harry asked. "Only one person knows what's in my locket. Only . . ."

That's when Spud started to undress. Or I should say, started to take off his potato suit.

First the mittens. Then the huge pants, with the padded behind, which fell to the floor of La Maison de Trash like the giant bean-bag chairs they used to sell. And then the potato shirt, which had hidden buttons like tiny potato warts all down the front. And finally the huge, ugly potato head.

We all couldn't believe who it was. Even Spud seemed shocked to find himself standing before us.

"Eric," said Harry.

"Eric," said me.

"Oh, Spud," said Jeanie.

"Your turn," said Eric to Harry.

Harry loosened his grip from the locket, and then, very deliberately, he opened it up with his beautiful fingers.

It was me in there. It was Rosie.

Epilogue

It turned out that Harry had liked me all along. *All* along. I'd like to be able to say that I'd known that. Otherwise, why would I have been chasing him the way I did? Why would I have been counting Harrys instead of sheep? I'm not the kind of girl who goes after boys who don't go after her. I mean, with my experience I know what I'm doing when it comes to boys.

But I *didn't* know. And yet I went right on making a fool of myself. That's a very wise thing to do. When you love someone who doesn't love you, or who you think doesn't love you, you learn a major lesson in life: *boys are nuts!*

Harry wasn't a nut. He would have been if he hadn't been in love with me. But he had been. Forever, I'm sure. Or at least since we first met when he was six and I was four.

But it's hard for a boy who's in love with his own face to

love a girl who's in love with her own face even if she's in love with his face, too.

Harry wasn't immune. Not to me, anyway. He was just hiding his feelings, exactly the way he hid that picture of me inside the President Reagan locket after he found it on the shelf where I put it when Mrs. Higgins took it my first day working at La Maison de Trash.

But everyone was hiding, weren't they?

I was hiding from my true potential for dating greatness every time I went out with a boy who was wrong for me.

Professor Stanislaus Fuller was hiding from his destiny when, come Christmas, the people who had rented him their house returned to claim it, and Stan said it was time for him to return to New York City.

I sat down with him and my mother and told them it was time for them to talk about getting married, if they hadn't already.

They looked at one another. I realized this was all that had been on their minds for months, and they hadn't said a word about it.

"Grow *up*, you two," I shouted. "Go for it, Mom! Go for it, Stan!"

They did.

We all did.

And Eric Levy was certainly hiding inside his potato suit (and what a waste of his impeccable features!).

Even Jeanie was hiding, by not telling Spud that he had to come out of his potato suit. Letting someone else hide from you is a form of hiding from yourself.

Jeanie was angry with Spud/Eric for a while. She felt Spud had played a terrible trick on her by coming around as Eric and trying to get her to go out with him and betray Spud.

"You were testing me," she said. "I don't like tests. Tests are for school. People who love each other don't give each other tests."

"But I wasn't really testing you," he explained. "I was testing myself. I wanted to see if you liked me."

"I liked you. You knew I liked you."

"No," he said. "I knew you liked Spud. Crazy, ugly Spud. But I got trapped in Spud. Don't you see? I was afraid that when you saw me as I really am, you wouldn't like me. So I thought I would have to wear that silly potato suit for the rest of my life. I wasn't trying to get you to betray Spud. I just had to find out if you liked me as me, Eric, instead of me, Spud."

"But you *are* Spud, Spud," said Jeanie.

"Please call me Eric," said Eric.

"Then you'll have to talk in that phony deep voice," Jeanie told him.

"Forever?" he asked.

"Forever," she replied.

Forever. And it didn't even matter what their Love-oscope might say.

But Jeanie finally learned to call Eric "Eric," no matter what voice he talked in.

For Christmas she gave him something she'd never been able to find, so she had to have it made up: a Spud license plate.

He put it on the left rear bumper of his car. On the right rear bumper was another license plate that said Jeanie.

They rode around, a mystery to everyone but themselves.

Harry and I were a mystery too, even though we all knew what our Love-oscopes said: we were going to get married and have children.

But I didn't believe in things like Love-oscopes and love potions. And neither did Harry. I thought. He just said he did.

But then we had our first real date. Neither one of us asked the other one. We just sort of agreed to do something. To do something together. And I guess that's what a date really is, when you get right down to it.

"So where do you want to go?" he asked.

"I'll show you."

He followed me as we rode our bikes out to Lake Wooneemonascetasket.

When we got there, I said, "That night you came out here—were you with a girl?"

"Yes."

"I knew it! You lied, Harry, you lied."

"No, I didn't."

"Sure you did. You said, 'Who said anything about a girl?' "

"Hey," he said. "I like that. You actually memorize things I say. That's amazing. I didn't think I ever said anything worth memorizing."

I thought about that for a moment. "Come to think of it, you haven't, Harry. *Bons mots* are not your strong point."

"I didn't take French," he said. "And I'm not big on giving candy to girls. You may not have noticed, but we carry no edibles at La Maison de Trash. Especially not candy."

"Who said anything about candy?"

" '*Bons mots*,' " he repeated, grinning.

Well, I never said I was in love with him for his sophisticated sense of humor. It was really his looks I loved. I'm not ashamed to admit it. In fact, after twelve years of knowing Harry, I hardly knew him. Except for his looks. Those I had memorized. They were actually part of my eyes. And if Harry were to be removed forever from my sight, in a certain way it would be the same as if he were right beside me, because I would never forget the way he looked, he would be part of my vision of the world.

And my vision of the world was what I was seeing right then—Handsome Harry Higgins's upside-down face as he rowed us across Lake Wooneemonascetasket and I lay stretched out in our rowboat with my head leaning against his knees.

"So who was the girl?" I asked.

"You."

"But I—"

"In my mind," he explained.

I'd never thought about Harry's mind before. But if he carried me around in it, even on lonely, solitary visits to Lake Wooneemonascetasket, then it was a mind I couldn't help but admire.

At one point, in the middle of the lake, Harry stopped rowing, bent over and tapped me on the shoulder.

"Yes?"

I thought he was going to ask permission to share our first kiss. But instead he said, "Here," and handed me a vial filled with a most beautiful clear blue liquid.

"What does it do?" I asked.

"It's for a boy to give to a girl to make the girl fall in love with him. And here's another one for a girl to give to a boy to make the boy fall in love with her."

"Do they work?" I asked.

"They're from La Maison de Trash, Rosie. Of course they work."

"You really love that place, don't you, Harry?"

"It's the whole world," he said.

I took the vials from him. I held them in my fingers. I put them up to my eyes and looked at Harry through the beautiful blue and pink light. And then I poured them both overboard.

"That's the last thing we need," I said, and we both laughed.

ABOUT THE AUTHOR

J.D. LANDIS is senior vice-president
and publisher at a major publishing company in New York. His most recent
young adult novel is *The Band Never
Dances*. He lives in New York City.